FRAMED

GORDON KORMAN

Scholastic Press • New York

For Michelle, the picture in my frame

Library of Congress Cataloging-in-Publication Data
Korman, Gordon.
  Framed / Gordon Korman. — 1st ed.
    p. cm.
  Summary: Griffin Bing is in big trouble when a Super Bowl ring disappears from his middle school's display case, replaced by Griffin's retainer, and the more he and his friends investigate, the worse his situation becomes.
  ISBN 978-0-545-17849-5 (hardcover)
  [1. Stealing — Fiction. 2. Middle schools — Fiction. 3. Schools — Fiction. 4. Friendship — Fiction. 5. Adventure and adventurers — Fiction.] I. Title.
  PZ7.K8369Fr 2010
  [Fic] — dc22

                                                              2010002583

       10 9 8 7 6 5 4 3 2 1   10 11 12 13 14

              Printed in the U.S.A.   23
              First edition, September 2010

          The text type was set in ITC Century.
          Book design by Elizabeth B. Parisi

I am a serious buyer for the valuable object that has recently come into your possession. If you are interested in making a lot of $$$, meet me under the Blind Justice statue in the lobby of the Cedarville courthouse. . . .

TWO WEEKS EARLIER . . .

1

A clammy rain misted down on the six hundred and eighty students assembled in ranks on the muddy front lawn of Cedarville Middle School. Soggy sneakers splashed as the principal led his students through twenty jumping jacks, bellowing encouragement through a megaphone.

Ben Slovak struggled along, trying to wave and jump while still keeping control of the wriggling lump in his hoodie. From time to time, a pointed snout and beady eyes poked up past his collar, looking distressed.

"I don't think Ferret Face likes this!" Ben exclaimed. Ben suffered from narcolepsy, a disorder where he might fall asleep at any time of the day. The small ferret inside his shirt was trained to administer a gentle wake-up nip whenever his patient began to drift off.

"Ferret Face is a smart guy!" puffed Griffin Bing, laboring beside him. "Yeah, okay, so we need a morning workout. But in the rain?"

Everyone knew that Dr. Egan had been a successful high school football coach before getting his doctorate in administration. But no one had expected the new principal to turn this middle school into training camp. It had been going on since the second day of the semester — push-ups, leg lifts, running in place, sit-ups.

Griffin was already more than sick of it — and he wasn't the only one. Out of the corner of his eye, he could see Logan Kellerman three rows over, barely going through the motions. Behind Logan, Melissa Dukakis thrashed on beneath a head of long, stringy hair that was now plastered to her face. She looked like the unopened bud of a tulip — one that was out of breath and puffing hard.

Of Griffin's closest friends, Pitch Benson alone was managing to keep up. Pitch was an accomplished rock climber in top physical condition. Her movements were fluid, her athleticism matched only by the principal himself at the front of the throng.

A painful slap made contact with the back of Griffin's head. He emitted a cry of shock, and his retainer popped out of his mouth and landed in the mud.

"Look alive, Bing!" sneered a nasty voice from behind him.

Under any other circumstances, Griffin would have stood right up to Darren Vader, his archenemy. But right now the priority was to save the retainer. His parents had made it clear that he was to guard the expensive dental appliance with his life.

He dropped down to his knees, scanning the wet grass. Where was it? All around him, flying feet stomped and flailed.

"Nobody move!" Griffin shouted.

"In your dreams!" Darren laughed, kicking mud all over Griffin's kneeling figure.

Desperately, Griffin ran his hands through the grass, feeling for the familiar plastic-and-metal shape. Nothing.

"Ben!" Griffin tried. "Can you help me find my retainer?"

"That's disgusting!" Ben exclaimed suddenly.

"What are you talking about?"

Ben was staring inside the collar of his hoodie. "Ferret Face just threw up on my stomach!"

"It might be motion sickness," offered Savannah Drysdale, who knew more about animals than anyone in town. "You know — the way people sometimes get nauseous on long car rides. Poor little guy. It's not his fault."

Ferret Face peered up out of the shirt with a grateful burp.

"But it's gross!" Ben complained.

Darren brayed a laugh. "Too bad they don't make little barf bags for ferrets!"

"Would somebody just help me find my retainer?!" Griffin wailed.

Savannah was disgusted. "Don't be such a baby. You're looking right at it." She reached down and plucked it off the turf. "If you keep your mouth shut for a change, maybe it won't fall out so often."

Griffin examined the filthy, slime-covered metal. Oh, how he hated this torture device! It squeezed, it scratched, it kept him up at night. But if he ever lost it, he would have to find a new family.

He turned and shook his fist at Darren. "Someday, Vader —"

He was interrupted by three sharp whistle blasts.

"All right, everybody!" Dr. Egan yelled. "Good workout. Remember, your mind can never be sharp if your body's not with the program. We'll make something out of you couch potatoes yet. Now listen up, because I've got big news."

An uncomfortable murmur rippled through the crowd. The students had heard more than enough "big news" in the past two weeks — like the big news that they were lumpy and out of shape, that soft bodies produced soft minds, and that sport was the ultimate character builder. They'd been told that homeroom would be replaced by twenty minutes of morning calisthenics — and that they were all going to get healthy, even if it killed them.

"The only news I want is that we don't have to do this anymore," Ben murmured.

"How come we can't hear his news inside, where it's nice and dry?" Savannah muttered under her breath as the rain turned to a steady drumming on their heads.

"If I catch cold," warned Logan, who had just landed the lead in the school play, *Hail Caesar*, "I won't be able to project my voice to the back row of the auditorium."

"How many of you know," Dr. Egan asked, "that Art Blankenship was a local boy from right here in town who graduated from this very school back when it was the old Cedarville High?"

Not a single hand went up.

"Who's Art Blankenship?" whispered Pitch.

Griffin shrugged and tried to clean off his retainer by wiping it on his pants.

"That's another thing we all have to learn!" the principal exclaimed. "Pride! Art Blankenship was the assistant linebacker coach of the nineteen sixty-nine Super Bowl Champion New York Jets! You'll never guess what I found behind a stack of toilet paper rolls in the custodial supply closet!" He held up a small, shiny object that no one could really make out. "This is Art Blankenship's Super Bowl ring! The real deal!"

There was a smattering of applause.

"His widow donated this ring in his memory to the old school, where he learned to become a winner!"

The applause grew a little stronger.

"You're right to be impressed," the principal approved. "But you should also be screaming your heads off! Somebody had no problem taking this treasure and sticking it on a dark shelf, to be buried in toilet paper and forgotten! Well, it's not forgotten anymore! This ring is going into a place of honor — in the display case in front of the office! Every time you see it, I want you to think about Art Blankenship's legacy — how he grew up here, and walked these halls, and went on to reach the highest possible level! Now, the bell's about to ring. I want to see some hustle and some pride as you go in for first period." He clapped loudly. "Let's move!"

He didn't have to give the order twice. There was a stampede for the door as the students rushed to get out of the rain.

Just as Griffin was about to step inside, the new principal barred his way.

"Griffin Bing, I'm not blind, you know. Do you think I didn't see you out there, goofing off, crawling around on the grass? Don't deny it. You've got mud on your knees."

"Sorry," said Griffin, reddening. "My retainer fell out, and I was having trouble finding it, what with the rain and all —"

"There are no excuses, only results," Dr. Egan interrupted impatiently. "It's true in football, and it's true in life. Don't think I don't know about you. Your reputation speaks for itself." From his pocket, he produced a neatly folded newspaper clipping from the *Herald*, Cedarville's local paper. The article read:

YOUTH CRIME WAVE IN "SAFE" CEDARVILLE?
By Celia White, Staff Reporter

We may think of youth crime as the problem of New York City and places like it. But how many of us are aware of our own little crime wave right here in sleepy Cedarville?

I'm not talking about mischievous doorbell ringing or unpleasant graffiti. That's kid stuff for our local "heroes." How about the theft of valuable zoo animals? Or a baseball card worth nearly a million dollars?

The police have so far decided to look the other way, so this paper is restricted by law from naming names. But the perpetrators are still among us, sitting in our classrooms, befriending our kids, and, for all we know, planning their next caper. . . .

Griffin looked up, too horrified to read on. The article was about him and his friends!

The principal fixed his piercing eyes on Griffin. "You're regular celebrities around here, you and your buddies."

"It's not true!" Griffin managed in a strangled voice. "I mean, it all sort of happened — but not like it's written there!"

How could he even explain it? Yes, he and his team had pulled off two zoobreaks and a baseball card heist. Yet what this football coach/principal could never understand was that, in all those cases, Griffin and the team had been fighting for *fairness.* Sure, a few laws had been broken, and the police had gotten involved. But none of the team members had ever been charged with any crime. In the end, the authorities had always been able to see that Griffin and his friends had only been trying to do the right thing.

"I'll let you off with a warning this time," Dr. Egan concluded. "But remember — I'm watching you. And make sure your accomplices know that I'm watching them, too."

Ben was waiting for Griffin in the main hallway. "What was *that* all about?"

Griffin burned with resentment. "It was about chewing us out for what we haven't done yet. Did you know that crazy old bat Celia White wrote an article in the *Herald* that pretty much calls us criminals?"

Ben flushed. "My mother reads Celia White every week. I just about lost an eardrum on that one."

"Yeah? Well, now it's Egan's new bible!" Griffin rolled his eyes. "The guy just made seven hundred kids do jumping jacks in a monsoon, and *we're* the ones who need watching? Celia White should be writing about that!"

Ben brushed nervously at the lump in his shirt where Ferret Face huddled. "We haven't been in middle school two full weeks and already the principal's out to get us."

Griffin nodded grimly. "We definitely need a plan to get him off our case. . . ."

He went on, but Ben had stopped listening after the fateful word: *plan*. In Cedarville, New York, Griffin Bing was The Man With The Plan.

And it always led to trouble.

NEW YORK JETS
WORLD CHAMPIONS

It was a heavy gold ring, designed to fit a very big finger. A large central diamond, surrounded by smaller diamonds, formed the shape of a football outlined in Jets green.

Melissa agitated her head, and her curtain of hair parted to reveal eyes wide with wonder. "You always hear about Super Bowl rings, but I've never seen one close-up before," she said in her quiet voice.

Pitch nodded, impressed. "Super Bowl Three was one of the greatest games in NFL history."

A jet of Windex hit the display case, and Pitch had to jump back to avoid being splattered.

Mr. Clancy, one of the custodians, reached a cloth over Pitch's shoulder and scrubbed at the glass in front of the ring. "Super Bowl Three was a joke," he muttered.

"But wasn't that the game where Broadway Joe Namath guaranteed victory and then made it happen?" Pitch asked.

"He got lucky," the custodian said sourly. "I was right about your age for that so-called Super Bowl. Worst day of my life." And he walked off, a Windex cloud obscuring the blue and white headband he wore at all times.

"I guess Mr. Clancy isn't a Jets fan," Savannah observed.

"I guess not," Pitch agreed. "But he's got to appreciate a real Super Bowl ring — that's pretty cool."

Griffin was disgusted. "Does it make you want to go out there and do more jumping jacks? This time in a blizzard? Or maybe a flood? Then we could burn extra calories by treading water!"

"All right, Griffin, we get it," soothed Ben. "You don't like Dr. Egan very much. Neither do I. You think I enjoy being barfed on by a ferret at eight o'clock in the morning?"

"At least you guys just have to deal with him at school," put in Savannah. "Try living across the street from the guy."

Pitch was appalled. "He's your *neighbor*? That's awful!"

"Everybody has to live somewhere, I guess," Savannah said unhappily. "Anyway, I don't see him around much. He's probably here all day, kissing his Super Bowl ring."

"It *is* something you don't see every day," Pitch admitted.

"It's nice," agreed Logan. "Not as nice as an Oscar, of course."

Darren came lumbering up, eavesdropping as usual. "The only Oscar you're ever going to touch, Kellerman, is the Mayer-wiener kind." He turned to Griffin. "How's the retainer? Got the swamp out of it yet?"

Griffin had just spent nearly twenty minutes rinsing the dental appliance under hot water. The last thing he was in the mood for was Darren's moronic sense of humor. But when he opened his mouth to fire off a retort, his retainer popped out again. He barely managed to catch it just before it hit the floor.

"Nice save," Darren sneered.

"Beat it, Vader."

"Dr. Egan told us to admire this ring and be inspired," said Darren, "and that's what I'm doing."

"Wait a second —" Griffin's eyes narrowed. "You *like* him?"

"Best principal on Long Island," Darren affirmed.

Griffin scowled into the display case. "More like Dr. Evil."

"We lucked out when we got him," Darren said smugly. "I'm the only seventh grader who made the football team, and I'm going to dominate!"

Pitch muttered something under her breath that no one could make out, which was probably just as well. For some reason, she'd been in a foul mood all week.

Darren beamed. "You guys are just bent out of shape because Dr. Egan will never let you get away with the kind of stuff you pulled in elementary school."

"Aren't you forgetting something?" Griffin could barely contain his anger. "You were there with us every step of the way — double-crossing us, stabbing us in the back —"

"Yeah — funny how it all got blamed on you

dopes, not me." The big boy peered through the glass of the display case at the Super Bowl ring. "I'm going to own one of these someday. Those are real diamonds! What do you think it's worth?"

"More than we could get for you," snapped Pitch. "Lard and hot air doesn't bring in much."

"It's not just the value of the diamonds and the gold," said a deep voice behind them. "It's the fact that it's so rare."

They turned to see Tony Bartholomew, a tall, serious eighth grader. "Every Super Bowl championship team has its own unique ring. Only the Jets and their coaching staff were given these. There are probably no more than fifty or sixty of them in the whole world." He paused. "And this one's mine."

That got their complete attention.

"How do you figure that?" Darren demanded.

"Art Blankenship was my grandmother's first cousin. That makes me his closest living relative."

"Except for his wife," Savannah pointed out. "And she gave the ring to the school."

Tony nodded his agreement. "But when the school tossed it in a dark corner somewhere, they were throwing it away. That's when it should have gone to me."

"Wow," said Logan. "What are you going to do?"

"I don't know," Tony said with equal parts dejection and determination. "Something. That ring belongs to me."

The bell rang, and the bustle in the hall grew louder. Tony melted into the crowd, and Darren took his leave with a cheerful "Later, losers."

Pitch shook her head in amazement. "Is it just me, or is this place even weirder than our last school?"

"I have a prescription ferret," Ben said with a sigh. "I'm not a good judge of weird."

3

A low growl issued from a set of jaws that would have fit a young *T. rex.*

Luthor didn't like computers. It was a holdover from the big Doberman's days as a guard dog in a collectibles shop — long nights locked in the store with only the power hum and the dim glow of the screen saver for company.

Griffin could feel hot breath on the back of his neck as he called up the e-mail on Savannah's monitor.

Dr. Egan —

It has come to our attention that your school's front lawn is located on a 3½ percent grade and is therefore UNFIT for Level Playing Field Activities (LPFAs) such as lawn bowling and morning calisthenics. Please suspend all LPFAs until the ground has been leveled and certified by a licensed engineering firm.

Sincerely,

The Coalition Against Repetitive Strain Injury

"That's the stupidest thing I've ever heard in my life," Savannah informed him.

"I have another one about how jumping jacks destroy ant habitats," Griffin offered.

"Okay, second stupidest. And if a kid can see that, Egan will spot it in a heartbeat."

"You're missing the point," Griffin insisted. "Yes, it's all fake. But it's just real enough that he'll have to check it out. The lawn *might* be sloped; the repetitive strain people *might* be real. How's he going to know unless he looks into it?"

"And how long is that going to take?" Savannah asked.

"Not long," Griffin admitted. "But we're going to give him hundreds of these things. Thousands, if we can think of them. And if he's busy twenty-four seven following up on our complaints, he won't have any time for his witch hunt against the kids Celia White says are ruining Cedarville."

"Yeah, but the message is going to be from *my* computer. He'll be able to see it's from me."

Griffin shook his head. "Melissa knows how to make an e-mail totally untraceable. She can bounce it twenty times around the world till it seems like it came from the president of Zambia. Let's see Dr. Evil try to give *him* a detention."

Savannah's eyes narrowed. "This is a *plan*, isn't it?"

"Of course not. This is more like a strategy. You know, a tactic —"

"That's the same thing!" she stormed. "I hope you're delirious, Griffin Bing! Have you forgotten what happened with the last plan? And the one before that?"

"Hey, I know it got a little hairy," Griffin said defensively, "but we came through it okay."

"Don't you remember what that cop said would happen if we broke the law again? He said, 'arrested, cuffed, fingerprinted, and prosecuted.' Those were his *exact words*. I know, because we've all been hearing them in our dreams for the past four months, three weeks, and six days, give or take a few hours."

"Egan's got no right to treat us like criminals

for what we haven't even done," Griffin said stubbornly.

"I agree with you. We all do. But not a plan. It's just too risky."

Outside, a motor roared to life. A familiar stout figure came into view across the street, walking behind a gas lawn mower.

"It's him!" exclaimed Griffin, his face darkening. "Dr. Evil really *is* your neighbor!" Griffin watched as the principal carefully maneuvered the mower, cutting perfectly straight lines into the front yard. "He treats his own grass like it's sacred ground, but has no problem sending hundreds of kids out to do jumping jacks on public property."

Savannah looked distracted. "You'd better go now, Griffin. I've got a lot on my mind. We have a rat."

Griffin's gaze traveled to the small rodent habitat where a collection of hamsters, gerbils, and white mice scurried about the maze of multicolored plastic tubes. Savannah's room was a regular menagerie. She also had cats, rabbits, turtles, a parakeet, a capuchin monkey, and an albino chameleon named Lorenzo.

"I mean a real rat." She was tight lipped. "Loose in the house."

When the truth dawned on Griffin, he couldn't hold back a peal of laughter. "You're *infested*? You? The animal expert?"

Luthor let out a bark that rattled the windowpanes.

"No offense," Griffin added quickly. "It's just that if there's anyone who could handle animal problems, I thought it would be you."

Savannah sighed. "Well, you're wrong. It hits us twice as hard as anyone else. The animals sense there's a stranger in the house. Tempers are short. The rabbits are bickering. The turtles haven't come out of their shells in days."

Griffin shrugged. "Call an exterminator."

Savannah's eyes shot sparks. "You mean a hired assassin who kills living creatures in exchange for money? I don't think so. Besides, poisons and traps don't discriminate. How would I keep the others safe?"

Griffin could see her dilemma. Savannah had devoted her entire life to loving, collecting, and caring for living creatures. To treat any animal as an enemy would be as difficult for her as flying to the moon.

He tried to lighten the mood. "Maybe you can send the rat across the street to Egan's house. I've got to get over to Logan's. Let me know if you change your mind about the e-mail."

> Dear Dr. Egan,
>
> As you probably know, the stage curtain in the auditorium squeaks, which is very distracting during set changes in the middle of a show. We have taken the liberty of picking out a new one from the Broadway Supply catalog. The cost is only $6000. Should we place the order and have them bill the school?
>
> Thanks!
>
> Friends of the Drama Club

Logan frowned. "There is no Friends of the Drama Club."

"Egan doesn't know that," Griffin told him. "And while he's finding out, he isn't making our lives miserable. The best part is Melissa will fix it so that no one will ever realize the e-mail came from you."

Logan was skeptical. "I don't know, Griffin. I've got my career to think about. I'll never make it in Hollywood with a criminal record. At least, not a boring one."

"That's why we have to do this," Griffin argued. "Dr. Evil's so convinced we're dirty that he's going to pin some rap on us sooner or later, even if we're totally innocent."

"Yeah, but if he finds out what we're doing, everything Celia White put in that article will be true," Logan reminded him. "The new curtain sounds great, though. Do you think we'll have it in time for *Hail Caesar*?"

Griffin held his head. "There *is* no new curtain!"

"But you said —"

"Just forget it. I'm going to see Pitch."

But Griffin found an even less receptive audience at the Benson house.

"Buzz off," Pitch told him. "I don't want to talk about it anymore. From now on, *plan* is a four-letter word."

"At least take a look at the e-mails," Griffin pleaded. "I've written some really classy ones for you."

Pitch would not be moved. "I don't care if they're all by Shakespeare. If Egan hates us as much as you say, the last thing we want to do is make him mad."

Griffin would not back down. "So it's totally fine for him to accuse us — not to mention turn the whole school into football workouts."

"Hey," Pitch snapped, "I *like* football. I like all sports. As a matter of fact . . ." Her voice trailed off, and she stared at the wall behind him, looking miserable.

"What?"

"Nothing," she mumbled evasively. "It's no big deal."

"What's up with you, anyway?" Griffin demanded. "You've been in a lousy mood for weeks! Since even before school opened, way back when Darren started bragging about . . ." His eyes widened. "Pitch — you tried out for football, didn't you? And you're upset because you didn't make it?"

"Worse." She studied her sneakers. "I went to that scrimmage. I was as good as anybody there. Not as big as Vader and some of the eighth graders, but faster and more athletic. Then Egan saw me. He wouldn't even let me on the field. He said girls can't play football — that I was just going to get hurt."

Griffin grinned. "You could press Vader into salami. I'll bet you told Egan that, too."

She did not share his smile. "He really is Dr. Evil, Griffin — and it has nothing to do with morning calisthenics or Celia White. The first game starts in a few hours, and it kills me that I won't be in it. I always believed there was no cliff I couldn't scale, no crag I couldn't beat. But being a girl — that isn't something you overcome with second effort."

"That's why you should be on board with this," Griffin argued.

"What's the point?" she replied listlessly. "Like there's anything he could do to me that would be worse than brushing me off like a piece of lint without even giving me a chance."

> Dr. Egan:
>
> We are writing in regard to one of your students, Benjamin Slovak. It has come to our attention that the calisthenics program at your school has been causing motion sickness in his pet ferret. . . .

Ben didn't even finish reading the message on the screen. "You said the e-mails were supposed to be anonymous."

"It's *about* you, not *from* you," Griffin explained reasonably. "It's signed the ASPCA, see?"

Ben wasn't convinced. "And everybody else said yes to this?"

Griffin chose his words carefully. "They will once you're on board."

"Why can't you just admit that *you're* the only person who wants to do it? Even Melissa said no, didn't she?"

Griffin knew a moment of doubt. Shy, with-drawn Melissa was usually so thrilled to have friends that she was an automatic yes. But this time he wasn't so sure about her. He thought back to her exact words: *I think I might be out*, she'd told him. *I want to be in, but I'd better be out.*

Aloud, he said, "You know Melissa — she'll come around eventually."

"It's different now," Ben argued. "We're done with second chances. You know, there are worse things in the world than jumping jacks in the rain."

Griffin looked totally defeated. "Then Dr. Evil *wins*."

"He was *always* going to win, Griffin. He's the principal. It's his game." All at once, Ben peered critically at his best friend. "Hey, man, did you forget your retainer?"

"No, I put it in this morning, same as —"

And then Griffin registered that the familiar pinching discomfort was no longer there. *"Oh, no!"*

The cry of alarm was so sharp that Ferret Face emerged from Ben's collar to investigate the disturbance.

Ben tried to be helpful. "Were you at anybody's house before you came here?"

"I was at *everybody's* house!" Griffin lamented. "It could have popped out anywhere!"

The hunt began. They scoured Ben's room and then retraced Griffin's steps from the front door and up the stairs. Next, the search followed the bike route to the Slovak home from Griffin's previous stop — Melissa's house. And from there they backtracked to the Bensons', the Kellermans', and the Drysdales'. There was no sign of the missing dental appliance.

Griffin was devastated. "I'm dead! I was so worried about Dr. Evil that I forgot about Mom the Merciless! When she finds out the retainer's gone, she's going to Krazy Glue my mouth shut!"

It wasn't an actual Krazy Gluing, but in a lot of ways it was even worse. Mom didn't holler; she played the "disappointed" card.

"We don't ask much of you, Griffin. In fact, we've probably cut you more slack than any other parents in America. But we have the right to expect a little responsibility. Why is it so difficult to keep a retainer in your mouth?"

"I might still find it," he offered. "Savannah says Luthor's a good tracking dog. They're going to help me look." He tried to sound more hopeful than he felt. Luthor was bred for combat, not search and rescue, no matter how much Savannah loved him.

"How am I ever going to tell your father about this?"

Griffin winced. When it came to the guilt trip, Mom was a travel agent. She went on and on about how expensive the retainer was, how vital it was to his health and the very shape of his face. The fact that he couldn't hang on to this one thing proved that he was irresponsible and untrustworthy. Worse, it showed that he took everything for granted and had no respect for the advantages he had in this world.

It probably would have gone on for hours, but he was saved by the doorbell — Savannah with the trusty Luthor at her side, looking more the size of a small pony than a dog.

"Well, I guess I'd better start looking," he said lamely.

"An excellent idea," Mrs. Bing informed him severely. "You can't be without it for very long. If it doesn't turn up in a couple of days, you'll have to be fitted for a new one. And rest assured that the cost will come out of your allowance."

At my pay grade, Griffin thought gloomily, *that'll take about eighty years.*

Aloud, he said, "I'm on it."

"We're looking for Griffin's retainer, sweetie." From her pocket, Savannah produced her old retainer and held it in front of the huge black eyes. "Like this."

She turned to Griffin. "Breathe on him."

"Why?"

"He needs to know the scent of the inside of your mouth," she explained reasonably. "That'll guide him to the retainer when we're close to it. Make sure you get right up to his nostrils."

"He'll bite my head off!" Griffin protested.

"Of course he won't," Savannah assured him. "He wants to help you."

Griffin regarded the gigantic head. A trickle of slobber traced a path along the expansive jawline. He leaned in and blew a quick puff of breath at Luthor's big snout.

"Closer," Savannah ordered. "Open your mouth so he gets a really good whiff."

Savannah considered Luthor the mildest, sweetest creature on earth. Griffin did not agree. One retainer and eighty years of allowance seemed a small price to pay to avoid being torn limb from limb.

But Mom's "disappointed" card wielded great power over him. He got in the Doberman's face, opened his mouth, and let out a long breath.

Luthor's loud bark traveled straight down Griffin's windpipe and vibrated his heart.

"Good boy, Luthor!" Savannah cheered. "Now let's find it!"

They retraced the route between the houses Griffin had visited, jogging to keep up with the Doberman's huge strides. He'd always rolled his eyes at Savannah's speeches about Luthor's intelligence and sensitivity, but the dog truly seemed to understand what they were doing. Luthor kept his snout low to the ground, sniffing the pavement, while Savannah whispered encouragement.

"Don't let him put it in his mouth when he finds it," Griffin said nervously. "Dog drool can contaminate a retainer forever."

Savannah shot him a disapproving look. "Don't be a baby. An animal's mouth is far more sanitary than a human's."

"Yeah, but grosser!"

As they passed the Kellerman house and headed toward the Bensons', Luthor's ears went up at the distant cheering noise.

Savannah pointed down the street to Cedarville Middle School. "It's the football team — their first game. Sounds like they got a big crowd."

"I wonder why," Griffin said sarcastically. "Dr. Evil has only been announcing it ten times a day."

As they approached the field, a familiar figure came into view. Pitch was perched thirty feet up a tree, watching the game over the crowded bleachers. Even from their worm's-eye view, Griffin and Savannah could see she was brooding.

"Who's winning?" Griffin called up to her.

"Who cares?" came the reply. But the young climber scrambled down the trunk to join them on the sidewalk. "Let's just hope Vader doesn't get a touchdown. We'll never hear the end of it."

Savannah was mystified. "Why can't you just watch from a normal seat?"

"I'm not giving Egan the satisfaction," Pitch growled. "If this game gets a good turnout, it's not going to be because of me." She peered at Griffin's mouth. "Any luck finding the retainer?"

"We still have a few more places to look," Savannah told her. "Come on, Luthor."

Pitch accompanied them. As they passed by the school, they got a view of the action on the field. The Cedarville Seahawks trailed 14–10, but the home team was driving. The huddle broke, and Darren noticed them as he took his place behind the quarterback.

He called, "Hey, losers!" and popped in his mouth guard.

That was all Luthor had to see. He took off, jarring the leash from Savannah's grasp.

Savannah read the dog's mind. "Come back, sweetie!" she called. "That's not the retainer!"

Luthor couldn't hear her over the roar of the crowd. Darren had put something in his mouth, and that needed to be investigated. He galloped onto the field like a racehorse.

"Darren — look out!" Savannah cried.

But Darren was completely focused on the play that was unfolding. He took the handoff, stutter-stepped behind a block, and broke through the line at full speed. The cheers of the crowd were an infusion of rocket fuel, energizing his legs. He was in the clear, sprinting for a go-ahead touchdown, with no defender in his path.

The tackle came from the place he least expected. A giant dog pounced on him from above, a monstrous black and brown body that momentarily blocked out the sun before flattening him to the turf. A huge paw reached under his visor and yanked his guard out by its tether. Powerful jaws snapped the plastic strap clean in two, and then the beast was gone as suddenly as it had appeared, taking the mouthpiece with it.

Pitch was wide eyed. "Too bad there's no highlight film for *that*!"

Luthor trotted back to Savannah and deposited the mangled mouth guard into her hand.

She patted his head ruefully. "It was a good try, sweetie."

Dr. Egan did not agree. He charged over, the entire Seahawks team at his heels. "Who let that dog on the —" He pulled up short when he recognized the three students with Luthor.

"It's all a big misunderstanding," Savannah explained reasonably. "Luthor saw Darren's mouth guard and thought it was —"

"I don't want to hear it!" the new principal yelled. "That was a deliberate attack!"

Griffin spoke up. "You can't blame Luthor, Dr. Egan —"

"I'm not blaming the dog — I'm blaming you three!" The principal turned his flaming features on Pitch. "*You* have a grudge against this team!" And on Savannah. "*You* have to control your pet!"

"He's not a pet, he's a family member —"

"And *you* —" The principal's rage was directed at Griffin now. "You're the ringleader of these juvenile delinquents, and this is where it ends! To train

34

an animal to attack someone is the same as using a weapon."

"What's going on here?"

A tall, birdlike woman pushed her way into the huddle and peered over her beak of a nose, panning from face to face. A notebook was shoved forward, pencil poised threateningly. "Who is responsible for setting that dog on this defenseless boy?" She placed a long, bony arm around Darren.

Griffin's heart sank. Of all the people who had to be at the football game to witness this — Celia White. He recognized her from the picture atop her weekly column in the *Herald*.

And she recognized him. "Griffin Bing — is this your dog?"

Savannah spoke up. "He's mine. And he hasn't done anything wrong."

The reporter produced a cell phone. "Why don't I call animal control and get their opinion? If I'm not mistaken, the law says a dog that attacks people has to be put down."

Savannah turned deathly white and swayed dizzily for a moment.

"Okay, okay," the principal announced. "Let's dial this back a notch. Nobody's getting put down." He looked daggers at Griffin. "Yet."

"What about my run?" demanded Darren, who was none the worse for wear except for a muddy jersey. "I was home free when the mutt pounced!"

The referee supplied the answer. "The play never happened. It was whistled dead for an unauthorized person on the field."

"It wasn't a person, it was a dog! And he owes me a touchdown!" Darren complained.

"Don't worry, young man," Celia White promised. "Everyone will know what was done to you — on Monday, when my column comes out, and I describe this incident in detail!" She glared at Griffin and bird-walked back to her seat in the bleachers, writing furiously as she went.

Dr. Egan reserved his anger for his students. "I want that dog and the three of you off my field now. And at school, if I see so much as a late slip from any of you, things are going to get ugly."

Griffin caught twin looks of dismay from his two friends. Things were already ugly.

And getting worse.

By Monday morning, the doomsday clock had ticked down to six hours. If the missing retainer did not magically reappear by the time school ended, an expensive replacement would have to be ordered.

"Otherwise, my teeth might start to get crooked again," Griffin called up the stairs of the Drysdale home. "To be honest, I'd rather have crooked teeth than deal with my mother anymore."

Mom was out of the vocally disappointed phase. Now she just sighed. It was amazing how much that woman could say without using words.

Griffin had stopped by Savannah's on the way to school, hoping that Luthor had come through over the weekend. If the Doberman could target Darren's mouth guard from twenty yards away, surely it was possible that he might stumble upon the real retainer.

"Sorry, Griffin, we haven't even had a chance to look." Savannah descended the steps, Luthor at her side. Cleopatra, her monkey, slid down the banister and jumped onto the dog's muscular neck. "The rat's still here, and it's a total nightmare. Lorenzo's turned pink — that's as red as you can get when you're albino." She swung her backpack over one shoulder.

Suddenly, Luthor let out a *woof* that made the rafters ring. He approached her and began pulling at the canvas bag.

"See how upset things are?" she pointed out to Griffin. "He's used to me going to school, but ever since the rat, they're all on edge. That's enough, Luthor. I'll be home soon."

The big Doberman began to whine. Cleopatra bounced and chattered in agitation. Their eyes never left Savannah's backpack.

Something about the bag was setting them off.

All through the school day, Dr. Egan's disapproving gaze seemed to follow Griffin wherever he went. He was relieved to get out of there — until he spied his mother in the car pool line. The doomsday clock had officially run out. It was time to order the new retainer.

Ben found him later that afternoon. Griffin was in his yard, struggling to pick up a giant armload of leaves. He staggered over to the lawn bag and jammed them inside, sending a good 50 percent fluttering back to the grass.

"You're alive." Ben stepped through the gate, Ferret Face poking out of his collar like a hood ornament.

"That's your opinion," Griffin said with a grimace. "Grab the spare rake and give me a hand."

"Won't your folks get mad if *I* do your punishment?"

"It's not punishment. It's the first installment of paying them back. I should be in the clear by Christmas, two thousand twenty-nine. Easter, the latest."

Ben picked up the second rake and began to work on a new leaf pile. "How mad was your mom?"

"Not bad. She's been so ticked off the whole time that she didn't have much anger left for today. She peaked early."

Ben deposited a rakeful in the open bag. "What about your dad?"

Griffin shrugged. "He's pretty distracted these days with the Vole-B-Gone."

Mr. Bing was the inventor of ultramodern fruit-harvesting equipment, like the SmartPick™ and the Rollo-Bushel™. His latest creation, the Vole-B-Gone™, was an electronic trap designed to protect trees from orchard pests.

"Your dad's a genius and all," Ben put in, "but after two great inventions, he was bound to come up with something that doesn't work."

"It works perfectly," Griffin countered. "Once the vole is in the cage, it triggers the sensor, and the door shuts in less than a tenth of a second."

"So what's the problem?"

"They won't go in," Griffin explained. "It's almost like they know what it's for. Dad's tried everything to attract them, but it's a no go. Who knew voles were so picky about where they hang out?"

Ben set down his rake. "I don't want to put you in an even worse mood, but the new *Herald* came today." He pulled the tabloid-sized paper from his backpack and handed it to Griffin. The headline blazoned:

VICIOUS DOG ATTACK ERASES WINNING TOUCHDOWN
By Celia White, Staff Reporter

The savage fury of the animal kingdom was unleashed upon an innocent middle school sporting event on Saturday. . . .

"Savannah isn't going to like this," Ben predicted mournfully.

Griffin scanned the article. Most of it decried Luthor as a danger to public safety, but the journalist had saved a special zinger for Griffin and his friends:

. . . While juvenile protection rules prevent this reporter from identifying the culprits, you can rest assured that the delinquents who trained the dog are the very same who have been responsible for local lawlessness in the past. Until we, the citizens of Cedarville, take a stand against this behavior, we can only expect more of it in the future.

"My mother thinks everything Celia White writes comes straight from the great truth oracle of the universe," Ben said glumly.

The Man With The Plan believed that kids could

and should stand up to the adult world. Yet a principal wielded absolute power in his school, and a reporter always had the last word.

Something had to be done.

But what?

Dark clouds loomed overhead when Griffin and Ben arrived at school the next day, but the threatening storm was mild compared to the thunderheads on Savannah's brow.

She was waiting for them outside the front entrance. "You won't *believe* who came to my house yesterday!" she seethed. "Animal control! They read Celia White's column! They think Luthor's dangerous!"

Griffin and Ben exchanged a pained expression. They agreed with animal control 1,000 percent, but they didn't dare admit that to Savannah.

Ben cleared his throat carefully. "Did they get a good look at him?"

"Of course!" She was indignant. "And those so-called animal experts couldn't see what a gentle creature he is. How could you gaze into those big, beautiful eyes and miss the kindness and compassion?"

Griffin shrugged off a strangled look from Ben and turned back to Savannah. "So what happens now?"

"We're allowed to keep him in the house and in the backyard so long as the gate is closed. But if he's caught outside our property, except in a full harness and a muzzle, he can be impounded. That's the word they used — *impounded*. Like he's a shipment of bad bananas from South America."

"Look at the bright side," Ben offered lamely as they entered the building.

Savannah wheeled on him furiously. "How could there be a bright side? Luthor is a strong, free, vital creature who needs open space to roam and explore! For him, this will be like a prison sentence!"

"Exactly," Ben explained. "Every single thing has gone wrong this year."

Griffin raised an eyebrow. "And that's the bright side?"

"Well," Ben reasoned, "you have to admit it would be pretty hard for life to get much worse."

A bloodcurdling shriek echoed throughout the building. All conversation halted in mid-word.

Everyone froze. There was sudden silence except for the thump of a few textbooks hitting the floor. Ferret Face popped up from Ben's collar, scanning his surroundings in alarm.

Heads turned in the direction of the noise. Hundreds of pairs of anxious eyes peered down the corridor that led to the office. The cry had been pure primal agony. What was happening at their school?

Ben turned white to the ears. "What was *that*?"

"Come on!" Griffin led the charge through the halls, dodging shocked students. They pounded past the cafeteria and rounded the corner toward the front entrance.

A crowd was already assembling at the main display case, pointing and speaking in urgent whispers. Mr. Clancy was there, holding back the swarm, perspiration trickling down to his blue and white headband.

Dr. Egan burst from the office in a state of high agitation. "Out of my way!" bawled the principal in an echo of the original scream. He waded through the throng and began to work at the lock on the glass panel, trying key after key from a large ring.

Griffin ran up. "What happened?" he asked a

tall student who seemed to have a good vantage point on what was going on.

It was Tony Bartholomew. "Somebody stole the Super Bowl ring," the eighth grader replied angrily. "*My* Super Bowl ring!"

"But how?" asked Ben, watching the distraught principal searching for the right key. "The case is locked up tight."

"Not my problem," Tony said grimly. "All I know is somebody owes me one Super Bowl ring."

At last, the principal was able to open the lock. He slid the panel aside and reached his hand in. Griffin wiggled to the front for a better view.

The view was clearer, but not better. It was true. Art Blankenship's Super Bowl ring was indeed gone. In its place on the black velvet was a small object — pink plastic and shiny silver wire. It was —

Griffin goggled. No. Impossible —

Dr. Egan's beefy hand closed on the item. He brought it out of the case and examined it. His wild eyes found Griffin in the crowd.

Griffin was in a state of shock. He stared at the piece, unable to believe his eyes.

"What is it?" whispered Ben, who was too short to see what the principal was holding.

"A retainer," said Griffin in a strangled

voice. Engraved on the plastic palate were five letters:

G. BING

"I want that ring back," the principal ordered. "Now."

"I don't have it." Griffin was barely able to conjure the breath to get any sound past his lips. "I didn't take it."

"How do you explain the retainer, then?" Dr. Egan demanded. "Since the first day of school, every time you open your mouth, that thing falls out. Well, you should have kept your mouth shut while you were stealing the ring! Because now your retainer proves that you're guilty."

"I'm not! The case was locked!"

"That wouldn't be a problem for an experienced burglar," the principal accused. "Locks have never stopped you before, have they?"

The Man With The Plan had been confronted with the unexpected many times. He'd been surprised, astonished, even blown away. But never had he been so completely and utterly blindsided to the point where he could not even find the words to defend himself. He stared at the retainer, incapable of believing his own eyes. He could barely work up any anger at Dr. Egan for putting the blame on him. With this kind of evidence against him, he almost blamed himself.

"I lost my retainer a few days ago," he managed finally. "Ask anybody. All my friends know."

"You mean your accomplices?" the principal challenged. "Not the most reliable witnesses."

"Somebody must have found it, and they did this to frame me!"

"All I know," Dr. Egan told him, "is that a major piece of sports history is missing, an item of jewelry worth tens of thousands of dollars. If you don't hand it over, I'm going to have to take this to the next level."

All Griffin could say was, "It wasn't me."

The principal addressed his students. "Everyone — back to your lockers. This doesn't concern you." His furious gaze fell on Ben and Savannah. Pitch, Melissa, and Logan inched forward to support their friend. "And I *certainly* hope it doesn't concern any of you."

He marched Griffin into the office and slammed the door.

"Lottie," he said to his secretary, "call the police."

It was not the first time that Detective Sergeant Vizzini had visited the Bing house. He had been there investigating the stolen Babe Ruth card and had also stopped by after the zoobreak incident.

His dark eyes panned the familiar surroundings of the kitchen. "New curtains. I like the color," he approved. "Brings out the wood stain of the cabinets."

"Thank you," said Mrs. Bing anxiously. It was an automatic response. Curtains were the last thing on her mind. "Officer, I know Griffin has had issues in the past. But this time he's telling the truth. His retainer has been gone a few days now — long before that ring disappeared."

Vizzini nodded. "I believe you."

Mr. Bing frowned. "Well, in that case, what are we doing here? Why is Griffin in trouble?"

"Here's the thing," the cop told them. "I believe that's what your son told you. Whether or not he told *you* the truth — well, that's a different matter entirely."

"No, it isn't!" Mr. Bing was triumphant. "We've ordered a replacement retainer. That's hard evidence! Just call the orthodontist to check."

"Already done." Vizzini flipped open a ring-bound pad. "The requisition left Dr. Torelli's office with the overnight paperwork after closing yesterday — just about the same time the burglary at the school must have taken place."

Griffin spoke up for the first time. "You think I went straight from a break-in to the *orthodontist?*"

"The office has late hours on Monday and Thursday," the detective read from his notes. "Yesterday's last patient didn't leave until — let's see — nine twenty-two p.m."

"That's crazy!" Mr. Bing exclaimed. "You don't order a four hundred–dollar dental appliance without taking some time to look for the old one first!"

"Unless you're trying to manufacture an alibi for the theft of something worth a lot more," Vizzini countered.

Mrs. Bing was bug eyed. "You're not just accusing him of a burglary! You're accusing him of using his own parents to cover it up!"

The detective leaned back in his chair, looking suddenly tired. "One of the first things they teach you in the police academy — you've got to see the big picture. You can't get locked into any one version of the crime."

"He's a twelve-year-old kid, not Al Capone!" Griffin's father exploded.

"A twelve-year-old who's already made a lot of so-called experts look like clowns. Me, for instance. Considering Griffin's past pattern of behavior, can you honestly rule out the possibility that he's responsible?"

The Bings hesitated.

Griffin was in agony. His parents *knew* the retainer had been gone since last week!

"I didn't do it," he said in a small voice.

"Maybe," the cop said evenly. "For one thing, I can't explain how you got into that display case. The lock shows no sign of tampering, and Dr. Egan insists he was in control of all keys. Does that mean it couldn't have been you? You're a resourceful kid, Griffin Bing. I underestimate you at my peril. And believe me, that's not a compliment."

"We stand by our son, Detective Vizzini," Griffin's mother said firmly.

The cop sighed. "Here's what happens now. We search your house for the missing ring. It should go pretty fast, since my men already know the place. In the meantime, Griffin has to stand before a judge —"

Mr. Bing looked alarmed. "Aren't you taking this a little too far?"

"Taking things too far," Vizzini replied, "is your son's trademark. Anyway, it's just a preliminary session to set a hearing date."

"That's even worse!" Griffin blurted.

Vizzini was unmoved. "Right from the beginning, a dozen different cops told you that one day your luck would run out. You think we were making it up? We're not that creative."

They were, however, punctual. Within the hour, six uniformed officers were riffling through drawers, tapping walls, searching cupboards, and running metal detectors along baseboards while the family waited out on the lawn.

"Well, Griffin, give us a heads-up," Dad said wearily. "Any chance they're going to find it?"

"Of course not!" Griffin snapped. "I thought you trusted me!"

"We *do* trust you," Mom soothed. "It's just that most parents don't even go through this once. Our street is starting to look like the parking lot of the police station."

"It's different this time," Griffin insisted. "Whatever happened to that ring, I had nothing to do with it."

The preliminary hearing was scheduled for the next day at ten a.m. Everything about the court-house seemed as if it had been designed to make Griffin feel small — the massive stone building, the towering marble columns, the security check-point, where uniformed guards directed visitors through a metal detector, like at an airport.

Police officers were everywhere, along with judges, jurors, lawyers, and people on trial, some even in handcuffs.

"I don't belong here," Griffin said to his parents. In the soaring atrium, his voice sounded high-pitched, like a four-year-old's.

"You don't have a thing to worry about," his father replied grimly. "You didn't take that Super Bowl ring, so all you have to do is tell the truth."

Dad was trying to sound upbeat and positive, but when he went off to ask directions to courtroom 235, he looked like a man marching to his own execution.

At last, they located the right room. Their lawyer was already there — Dalton Davis of Davis, Davis, and Yamamoto. He looked like Griffin felt — very dark and very serious. Together, the four of them spent the longest forty-five minutes of Griffin's life on a hard, wooden bench, waiting their turn to appear before the judge.

It wasn't much like the legal dramas Griffin had seen on TV. There was no prosecutor, no witnesses. In fact, the only other people there were Judge Koretsky herself and a stenographer with lightning fingers who typed every single word, including *ahem* and stomach gurgles.

Judge Elaine Koretsky was an incredibly compact woman, probably in her midfifties. Despite her small size, though, she radiated power and a no-nonsense attitude. She spent a few minutes glancing at papers in a file folder before turning her attention to Griffin. "Why don't you tell me your version of what's happened here?"

"Well," Mr. Davis began, "as I hope we've established —"

"I'd prefer to hear it from Griffin," the judge interrupted.

It was the umpteenth time Griffin had told this story. He should have had it letter-perfect by now. But he began to falter as he watched the judge's deepening frown.

When he was finished, she asked the one question he had no answer for: "So how did your retainer wind up inside the locked case where the ring used to be?"

"I can't explain it," he admitted, his face crimson. "I only know I didn't put it there."

The judge was not unkind, but her words fell like bombs. "You are convincing, but so is the evidence against you — especially in view of your past pattern of behavior."

"Griffin has never been convicted of a crime," Mr. Davis put in quickly.

"Maybe not," she returned, "but he's a regular trivia question in the police department quiz bowl league. I'm setting a hearing date for October twenty-ninth. If that ring should happen to turn up before then, it would make all our lives a lot easier. Especially yours, Griffin."

Griffin could only shake his head.

"In the meantime," Judge Koretsky went on, "I'm

notifying the school district that you are being removed from Cedarville Middle School. Until this matter is resolved, you will be attending the JFK Alternative Education Center."

Griffin was aghast. "You mean *Jail For Kids*?"

The judge glowered disapprovingly. "It's not jail. I've seen jail. You don't want to see it, too. JFK is the alternative program for secondary school kids in the county. Its students are there for various reasons — educational, social, behavioral, and legal."

Mr. Bing stood up. "What happened to innocent until proven guilty?"

The judge smiled. "That still counts. This isn't a sentence. I think it's a good idea to take Griffin out of the atmosphere where his problem is percolating."

"What about all my friends?" Griffin protested.

"Perhaps you could use a rest from them as well. And vice versa." The crack of the gavel made it official. "We're adjourned until October twenty-ninth."

8

Even Ferret Face, peeking out from Ben's collar, wore a woebegone expression.

Griffin and Ben, best friends since kindergarten, stood on the corner, waiting for the JFK bus to shatter their unbroken streak of attending the same school.

"Jail For Kids," Ben mourned. "I never thought one of us would have to go there. Alcatraz, maybe, but not JFK."

His attempt at humor got not even a smile from Griffin. "I can't believe this! It's so unfair! The whole point of living in America is so this can't happen to a person!"

They were joined at the bus stop by another JFK student, obviously a high schooler. He was six foot four with a full beard and a tuft of chest hair emerging from his shirt. Short, slight Ben felt the sun blocked out by the sheer bulk of him.

The newcomer regarded them without much interest. "New victims?"

"Just him!" squeaked Ben, pointing at Griffin.

The towering high schooler gave Griffin a once-over. "I've got zits bigger than you."

"It's a mistake," Griffin mumbled. "I'm not supposed to be here."

"Yeah — me, neither. I was innocent. All six times."

Griffin and Ben each took a step back and nearly tumbled off the curb into the road.

Ben leaned close to his friend. "You know what's the weirdest part of all this? How your lost retainer ended up where the ring was supposed to be. Have you thought about that?"

"Are you kidding? I've thought about nothing but. That's why nobody believes me — because they can't understand how it could have happened if I didn't do it."

"Well, how could it have happened?"

"I was framed."

Ben just stared at him.

"You know — framed! Set up! Railroaded! Whoever stole that ring found my retainer

58

and planted it in the display case so I'd get the blame."

Ben was wide eyed. "But who?"

"I haven't figured that out yet," said Griffin. "But I will. That's a promise."

Both were amazed when a regular yellow school bus rattled up to the stop.

Their companion was amused. "What were you expecting? A prison transport?"

With a last desperate look at his best friend, Griffin followed the bearded high schooler aboard.

The door slapped shut, and the vehicle roared away, leaving Ben on the sidewalk, awash in guilt. At this terrible moment, all he could think of was how grateful he was that *he* wasn't the passenger en route to Jail For Kids.

The John F. Kennedy Alternative Education Center was housed in the old Cedarville Public Library and served 187 students from the seventh through twelfth grades.

It would be wrong to say that every single kid was a juvenile delinquent. There was a variety of students with special needs, and some who simply had trouble getting along in regular school. But for the most part, the rumors about this place were true. It was the dumping ground for the worst of the worst in the county.

Griffin had expected to hate it. He just hadn't expected to hate it this much. He was the youngest, and the smallest, and the weakest — although there were no bullying problems at JFK. The teachers were tougher than the students, and they seemed to be everywhere, like spies. He witnessed a fistfight on day one. Before the first punch landed, there was a teacher on each combatant, pulling them apart. It was almost like the faculty knew what you were going to do even before you decided to do it.

Classes were a joke. The teachers cared only about keeping order, and the students didn't care about anything at all. At any given time, a third of them were asleep. The only question ever asked was "Can I go to the bathroom?"

If I'm stuck here for long, I'm going to end up stupid. . . .

That thought was replaced by an even darker one. If he was convicted of stealing the Super Bowl ring, then JFK would be Disney World compared with the juvenile detention center that awaited him somewhere.

When did life suddenly become such a nightmare?

It didn't really matter that they weren't teaching anything, because he was far too uptight to concentrate. He had to stop this runaway train. He was The Man With The Plan! He had better use this free time to work out a strategy to clear his name.

He opened his notebook to a blank page — they were all blank — and jotted a title across the top:

OPERATION JUSTICE

OBJECTIVE: To find out who FRAMED me.

List of SUSPECTS:
(i) . . .

Suddenly, the paper was ripped out of the notebook. The next thing Griffin knew, a paper airplane was sailing across the room toward the teacher.

Without thinking, he was up and chasing it through the aisle. Two people tripped him as he ran, but somehow he held it together, grasping frantically at the missile. No one must find evidence that he was working on a plan. He was in enough trouble already.

His foot came down in the wastebasket. The wipeout would have been spectacular, but the teacher caught him with one hand and the airplane with the other. It got a halfhearted cheer from the class — by far the greatest show of enthusiasm Griffin had seen all day at Jail For Kids.

Like most of the JFK faculty, Mr. Huber was 10 percent teacher and 90 percent prison guard, hard-muscled and tough. He hauled Griffin's foot out of the garbage, dropped the crumpled paper airplane in its place, and uttered a single word: "Sit."

"But I was just —" As he scanned the room, Griffin realized he had no idea who had done this to him.

"Sit," the teacher said again.

He didn't dare work on his plan now. So he shifted his mind into neutral and listened to the lesson for the remainder of the period. He remembered it from fifth grade. Maybe fourth.

At least there was one thing to be thankful for: No one had noticed the contents of the page that had become the paper airplane.

Or so he believed.

"Hey, Justice," came a voice from behind him in the hall.

Griffin kept his eyes straight ahead and hurried toward his next class.

"Yo — new guy. I'm talking to you."

Oh, no. Griffin turned around to face a squat bulldog of a boy, shorter than he was, but out-weighing him by at least thirty pounds. The kid resembled a sawed-off bodybuilder with a neck like a tree stump and a crew-cut cement block for a head.

"Pardon?" asked Griffin, not wanting to start anything with this mass of brawn.

"Operation Justice — what's the story?"

"I don't know what you're talking about," said Griffin stiffly. He wasn't about to waste words on the person who had stolen his paper and sailed it across the room.

"I'm talking about how you got framed," the boy insisted. "You and everybody else here. Think about it — a whole school for people with prob-lems, but nobody really deserves to be here. They were all framed, just like you."

Go away, Griffin prayed, focusing his eyes on a spot on the wall over the expansive shoulders.

The big stranger fell into step behind him. "Now take me, for instance. I'm the only inmate who actually belongs here. Everything on my record is totally true. I'm a bad person. What can I do?"

You can go away and leave me alone, Griffin thought. But he was too intimidated to say it.

The boy jumped in front of him. "Sheldon Brickhaus. My friends call me Shank — or they would, if I had any." He grasped Griffin's hand and squeezed with crushing force.

"Hey, that hurts!"

Shank grinned and tightened his grip. "Aren't you going to tell me *your* name?"

"Griffin. Griffin Bing."

"Good to meet you, Griffin Bing." Shank held on for a good ten seconds longer.

When Griffin finally got his hand back, red and throbbing, he mumbled, "I have to get to English now."

"English? Great. I'm going to the same class. There aren't a lot of middle school kids here. I bet we'll be together all day."

"Probably," Griffin agreed, trying to keep a mournful note out of his tone.

What was worse than being ripped from your

life and dumped into a place where you didn't know a soul?

Answer: Making "friends" you didn't want.

Thankfully, Griffin still had his real friends. When Jail For Kids was mercifully over for the day, he gathered the team in his garage. They sat in the shadow of a dozen different versions of the Vole-B-Gone, which lined the shelves and cluttered the workbench.

Pitch frowned at the wire-mesh enclosures as Griffin ushered the team members inside. "No offense to your dad, but I think the birdcage has already been invented."

"They're not for birds; they're for voles," Griffin explained. "Every year, hundreds of orchards lose their crop thanks to vole problems."

Savannah, the animal lover, regarded the traps disapprovingly. "I hope they're humane. Just because you're a pest, it doesn't mean you should have to suffer."

"Except for Darren," Ben added. "Anyway, don't worry about these traps. Griffin's dad says no vole will go near them."

Griffin cleared a space on the workbench and placed a sheet of paper where everyone could see it.

OPERATION JUSTICE

OBJECTIVE: To find out who FRAMED me.

List of suspects:
(i) Dr. Evil
Motive: worships the ring and hates me. Stealing it gets him exactly what he wants – the ring + me out of his hair. Also, has key to display case.
(ii) Darren Vader
Motive: notorious money grubber. Has talked about how much the ring must be worth. Also knew about retainer + as football player, has access to the school after hours.
(iii) Tony Bartholomew
Motive: believes the ring is rightfully his. Needs to blame me to distract attention from himself as a suspect.
(iv) Celia White
Motive: stealing ring proves that her columns about youth crime are true. Possibly eyeing better job at bigger newspaper.

"Wow." Logan whistled, impressed. "Which one do you think did it?"

Pitch rolled her eyes. "If we knew that, they wouldn't be called suspects, would they? My money's on Vader. He'd sell his own mother for a buck!"

"Darren's a saint compared to Celia White," said Savannah with an expression of distaste. "A person who would call animal control on Luthor is capable of anything."

Melissa agitated her head, allowing her beady eyes to emerge from behind her curtain of hair. "How *are* we going to find out which one of them is guilty?"

Griffin had thought they'd never ask. "I have a plan."

Nobody wanted a plan. But Griffin was in trouble when he had done nothing wrong. He was going to get all the support they had to offer.

"All right, Griffin." Ben sighed. "Lay it on us."

Ferret Face buried his head under Ben's shirt, as if he couldn't bear to listen.

"It's a sting operation," Griffin announced.

"We're going to use *bees*?" asked Logan, wide eyed.

"It means we trick the bad guy into revealing himself," Griffin explained.

"Or *her*self," Savannah amended, still thinking of Celia White.

"But how do we do that?" Pitch persisted.

"Why does anybody steal a valuable Super Bowl ring?" Griffin mused. "The suspects may have different motives, but there's one common denominator: money. So all we have to do is pretend to be buyers. We send all four of them an anonymous e-mail offering big bucks for the ring. We set up a meeting, and whoever comes must be the guilty one."

"Aren't you forgetting something?" Ben pointed out. "The suspects know us. Whoever comes to the meeting, the minute they spot us, meeting over. They'll take off and we'll never be able to prove they had the ring."

"I thought of that," said Griffin. "The meeting has to be at the courthouse where I had my hearing. There's a metal detector at the front door, and there's no way a big gold ring is going to make it through without setting off the machine. So the guilty party will have to take the ring out of his pocket and pass it through the X-ray machine. Then we've got him."

"Or her," Savannah added.

Pitch looked surprised. "You know, Griffin, I

always thought your plans were pretty lamebrained. But this is kind of smart. I mean, it could work."

"It better," said Griffin fervently. "I have less than a month to prove that I'm innocent."

I am a serious buyer for the valuable object that has recently come into your possession. If you are interested in making a lot of $$$, meet me under the Blind Justice statue in the lobby of the Cedarville courthouse on Friday at 5:30 p.m. Bring the hardware for a SUPER deal.

"It's perfect," Griffin approved, making shy Melissa blush. "Have you got the e-mail addresses for the four suspects?"

She nodded, hands caressing the keyboard. "All ready to go. I'm sending it through a dummy server in Malta. There's no way anybody could trace it. Even a computer expert would take years." Her finger hovered over the mouse. "Ready?"

"Let me do it, Melissa."

Griffin sent the e-mails himself. It felt important for him to start this plan personally, setting in motion the mechanism that would get him his life back. So far, things had just happened to him. He was a ping-pong ball, bounced around by forces he had no control over. Now he was fighting back, taking charge. It felt good.

The hardest part was waiting for Friday. Griffin moved like a zombie through the halls of Jail For Kids. His body may have been in this terrible place, but his mind was lost in the details of Operation Justice: Where should the lookouts be stationed with their walkie-talkies? What were the best vantage points from which a camera might capture the ring as the guilty party revealed it before the metal detector?

"Hey, Justice — over here!"

Griffin stood at the end of the cafeteria line, holding his tray at eye level so he could pretend not to notice Sheldon Brickhaus waving him over to a corner table.

Just keep walking. You don't see him.

But it was no use. He could already hear Shank's size-fourteen construction boots pounding in his direction. Next would come a playful punch that could flatten a bull, or "noogies" from knuckles of steel. It had been the pattern all week. There was no getting away from the guy.

"What are you, deaf?" Shank grabbed Griffin's earlobe and yanked.

Griffin's tray tilted, and 60 percent of his lunch

slid off onto the floor. He joined Shank at his table. What choice did he have? There was no mistaking it — Shank was no ordinary bully like Darren Vader. He was more like a cat playing with a captured mouse, getting maximum enjoyment before killing it. This torturer wasn't interested in wedgies or shaking you down for lunch money. For him this was sport.

Shank talked like they were best friends, but pain was never far away, coming in the form of vice-grip handshakes, bone-cracking backslaps, and assorted squeezes, tugs, and pinches. The fact that it didn't happen very often made it all the more horrible. The anticipation was enough to drive a person crazy.

Shank was an eighth grader, a year older than Griffin, but they shared five out of seven classes. The middle school kids were kept together as much as possible to separate them from the high schoolers. Not that classes made much of an impression on Shank. The squat, heavyset boy spent most of his time giving Griffin "friendly" advice on staying safe from their fellow students. Too bad he didn't have any pointers on staying safe from Sheldon Brickhaus.

"See that kid over by the tray return? His tattoo says 'murderer' in Farsi. Check out his backpack. It used to belong to a dead guy."

Griffin's eyes narrowed with suspicion. "What dead guy?"

Big shrug. "How should I know? He's dead, isn't he? And look at the punk rock girl with the blue hair. She's a gangster."

"No way!"

The shrug again. "Well, either that or she has a really bad attitude."

"Everyone around here has a bad attitude," Griffin reminded him. "You have the worst attitude of all, remember? You're proud of it."

"Well, in my case it's kind of a family tradition," Shank explained. "We get it from my dad. He's in nuisance wildlife removal. He spends all day facing down bats, skunks, and raccoons. Then he comes home and passes all that sunshine and roses on to the rest of us. I'm sure it's the same with your old man, right?"

Griffin thought of his parents, who were up nights worrying and meeting with lawyers, all to protect their son from the injustice that seemed to be swallowing him up.

"Yeah, all families are alike, I guess," he said aloud. So what if it wasn't true? With any luck, after Friday, he would never have to exchange another word with Sheldon Brickhaus.

OPERATION JUSTICE – PEP TALK

1st Draft
"My friends, the great challenge that lies before us . . ."

2nd Draft
"When unfairness rears its ugly head, we must . . ."

3rd Draft
"Guys, we have to make this work! I'm drowning at JFK. . . ."

Normally, Griffin knew exactly what to say at the moment a plan was put into action. But nothing was normal about Operation Justice. It was too personal, too serious. When the team met at the rendezvous point in front of the courthouse, all he could think of was: "Let's get this done."

Logan Kellerman donned his sunglasses, crammed his hat over his head, and promptly fell down the marble steps.

Griffin and Pitch rushed to rescue him.

"What's the matter with you?" Pitch hissed. "You're calling attention to us!"

"It's the sunglasses," Logan complained. "They're so dark!"

"They have to be dark," Griffin explained urgently. "The suspects could recognize us, especially Dr. Evil and Vader."

Logan got up from the sidewalk and dusted himself off. "How about a little sympathy," he complained. "I could have hurt myself, you know. If I fracture my skull, I'm pretty much out of *Hail Caesar.*"

"Get to your stations!" Griffin ordered.

Logan, Savannah, and Melissa climbed the stairs and slipped into the building.

Pitch, the advance lookout, crossed the street, selected a tall sycamore tree, and expertly shinnied up the trunk. Perched near the top, she waved with her binoculars to signal that she was in position.

Ben pushed Ferret Face out of view and assumed the other lookout spot at the base of the stairs, off to the side, behind some bushes.

Griffin slipped the walkie-talkie out of his pocket and held it to his ear. "Pitch — Ben — do you read me?"

"Loud and clear," reported Pitch. "I've got a perfect view up here. Whoever it is, I'll spot the jerk a block away."

"I'm good, too," said Ben.

"Check," Griffin replied. "I'm going in." He passed through the heavy revolving door and felt a chill that had nothing to do with the courthouse's oppressive air-conditioning. This was not a happy place for him. On his last visit to this building, he'd been exiled to Jail For Kids.

Put your emotions aside. You've got a job to do.

It was five o'clock, so the courthouse was busy. The day shift was leaving, and there was a lineup at the security checkpoint of employees and visitors for the evening court sessions.

It was good, Griffin decided. Just crowded enough so that he and his team wouldn't get noticed hanging around until their suspect arrived — an excellent environment for a sting operation.

He nodded at Savannah and Logan, who were already in line to pass through security, watching as they took their cell phone cameras from their pockets to run through the X-ray. With those two inside the checkpoint and Melissa and Griffin outside, surely one of the four of them would be able to snap a photograph of the culprit handling the ring. That would be all the evidence Griffin needed.

Now there was nothing to do but wait. It was 5:10 — twenty minutes to zero hour.

"All assets in place here," he murmured into the walkie-talkie.

"Ow!" came a voice on the other end. Griffin knew from experience what that meant. Ben had dozed off, and Ferret Face had delivered a small nip to wake him up again.

"Everything's fine," Pitch confirmed. "You know, Griffin, I can see your house from here."

"Keep your eyes on the courthouse," Griffin advised. "It's almost time."

"Got it — wait a minute! Red alert!"

"A suspect? Who?"

Pitch sounded disgusted. "Who else? Vader."

"I knew it!" The crime unfolded in Griffin's mind: Darren, stumbling on the lost retainer and instantly coming up with a scheme to steal the ring and blame it on his archenemy.

Revenge is going to be sweet!

He gave the signal — three sharp sneezes in a row. The team came to attention, hands on the phones in their pockets.

Griffin's concentration was broken by Ben's voice: "Red alert!"

"I know," whispered Griffin. "Vader's coming."

"No!" Ben insisted. "It's Celia White!"

"Make up your minds, you guys! Who is it? Darren Vader or Celia White?"

"Oh, man, it's *both*!" Pitch exclaimed. "Vader off the street, Celia White from the parking lot!"

Griffin gave three more sneezes. He wasn't sure if he was communicating that this was a new alarm, not a repeat of the first one. But he had to do something.

"Gesundheit," said the security guard at the X-ray machine.

Griffin melted into the crowd as Darren entered the building and got into line at the checkpoint. Within thirty seconds, Celia White was there, too, a couple of places behind Darren.

Griffin caught a bewildered look from Melissa, who was the only team member not wearing sunglasses. It seemed pointless to cover eyes that were always covered by hair anyway. But now those eyes were exposed and double-wide. The plan had not considered the possibility that more than one suspect might show up.

There was no time to think about that now. Darren was going through the checkpoint. The four photographers clutched their phones and edged closer.

Griffin watched breathlessly as Darren emptied his pockets and placed the contents in the tray. A few coins and — what was that? A flash of bright metal! He aimed the cell phone, ready to shoot.

A house key. False alarm.

He watched in dismay as Darren passed through the metal detector. Nothing. Not a peep.

Okay, it's Celia White, then. And Darren came only because the e-mail mentioned money, and he was hoping some of it might stick to his greasy fingers. . . .

Yet, minutes later, the reporter placed her pocketbook on the conveyor belt and breezed through the checkpoint without incident. Griffin almost broke his neck to get a view of the X-ray readout. Car keys, a BlackBerry, assorted junk, nothing more.

By now, Melissa's eyes were wide as saucers, and all sunglasses were trained on Griffin. Two suspects, no ring. What now?

Ben's voice came over the walkie-talkie. "Well, Griffin, which one was it? Darren or Celia White?"

"Neither!" rasped Griffin.

"Neither?"

"They both made it through security. They're clean."

"But how could that be?"

Pitch's voice provided a possible answer. "Red alert!"

"Oh, come on!" Ben exploded.

"Another one?" Griffin hissed.

"The Bartholomew kid," Pitch confirmed. "Heading for the stairs."

Griffin was so relieved that he almost forgot to sneeze the signal. All right — Darren was here for the money, Celia White for the story. Tony was the one.

The team watched as the gangling eighth grader — Art Blankenship's nearest relative — worked his way through the line and stepped into the metal detector. Griffin's grip tightened on the cell phone camera in his pocket. But no alarm disturbed the elevator music in the lobby. Tony didn't have the ring, either.

Griffin was devastated. Where had the plan gone wrong? Had he missed something?

And then the final red alert came over the walkie-talkie.

"It's Dr. Evil!" Ben rasped. "And he's got to have the merchandise! He's the only one left!"

"Watch yourself!" added Pitch. "This is it!"

Griffin felt his entire body tighten in apprehension as the principal entered the courthouse.

I should have known it would come to this!

There had been reason to suspect the others, but Dr. Egan was his true enemy — the man who had targeted him from the beginning and banished him to Jail For Kids.

The principal looked restless and annoyed, and stared pointedly at the Blind Justice statue beyond the checkpoint. If there were any question as to why he'd come, he clutched a printout of the untraceable e-mail in his hand.

Frowning impatiently, he stepped into the metal detector. The alarm was high pitched and piercing.

The team converged from the four corners of the atrium, cell phones out, shutters at the ready.

"Take a step back, sir," droned the security guard. "Put your keys, coins, and metal in the tray and try again."

The principal reached into his pocket.

Griffin stiffened like a pointer. This was it! In another second, the ring would be right in the open! He brought up the camera and leaned into the checkpoint.

Too close.

"Griffin Bing?" Dr. Egan exclaimed.

"Griffin Bing?" echoed another voice behind them.

Griffin wheeled. An all-too-familiar compact figure stood on the exit side of the checkpoint. Judge Koretsky.

Trapped like an animal, Griffin did the only thing he could think of. He brought the cell phone to his ear and said, "Hello?"

Angrily, the principal waved the e-mail printout at him. "Is this your doing?"

"I'd be very interested to hear the answer to that." Celia White, notebook in hand, leaned back over the divider.

Darren and Tony looked on from behind her, Darren with a self-satisfied smirk. There was nothing he enjoyed more than watching Griffin crash and burn.

At that moment, the walkie-talkie crackled to life with Ben's anxious voice. "What's happening, Griffin? Did it work?"

The answer to that, Griffin thought with a sinking heart, was a resounding no.

At least this time, Griffin didn't have to be hauled into court. He was already there.

He sat with his mother and Judge Koretsky in chambers, cringing under the evil eye that was coming in stereo.

"Why would you do such a crazy thing?" Mrs. Bing demanded.

"It was a sting operation," Griffin tried to explain. "No one believes I didn't steal the ring, so I have to flush out the person who did." He turned accusing eyes on the judge. "And it worked perfectly! Why didn't you search Dr. Egan when I told you to?"

Judge Koretsky's reply was icy. "We don't conduct unconstitutional searches on the say-so of a twelve-year-old."

"But he had the ring!" Griffin insisted. "That's what set off the metal detector!"

"That metal detector is set off fifty times a day by people who forget to remove their car keys or their cell phones."

"But it *had* to be the ring!" Griffin struggled to convince her. "The other three suspects breezed through. Dr. Egan was the only one who beeped! He took the ring to frame me, and now he's trying to sell it! It's a legal slam dunk!"

The judge glared across her desk. "When it comes to the law, I'll keep my own counsel, thank you very much. Now that we've heard your theory, maybe you should listen to mine: You concocted this whole thing to learn the value of the stolen Super Bowl ring so you'll know how much to ask for when you find a buyer."

Griffin turned pale. "But that's not true!"

"When the time comes, this court will determine what's true and what isn't. Meanwhile, I'm going to put a stop to your ability to engage in this outrageous behavior. As of this moment, you are under house arrest. You may leave your home only for school and medical or court appointments."

"But how am I going to clear my name?" Griffin blurted.

The judge was sympathetic but firm. "If you are truly innocent, the system will discover it." She turned to Mrs. Bing. "I'm relying on you to see to it that your son obeys this ruling. I'd rather not have to direct the police to enforce it."

"You won't have any more problems with Griffin," Mrs. Bing promised. "I'll get him straight home."

As they left the courthouse, Griffin turned to his mother. "Thanks for not calling Dad."

"Oh, I called him," she replied. "He's on his way back from the big library in New York City. He's interrupting his vole research to see if he can talk some sense into you. Fat chance."

"What choice did I have?" Griffin demanded. "Nobody believes I'm innocent!"

"You're innocent of stealing the ring. Dad and I have faith in that. But this foolishness today? You're one hundred and ten percent guilty! And God only knows who else you've dragged into it. If I call Estelle Slovak, is she going to tell me Ben was in his room doing homework at five thirty?"

Griffin remained silent. That was the one thing that had gone right. The rest of the team had managed to avoid being caught up in this disaster. It had been a classic Code Z — the moment when a plan was broken beyond repair. At least his friends were in the clear.

"Don't you see?" Mom went on. "When you pull a crazy stunt like this, you make yourself look guilty even if you have an airtight alibi!"

"Well, what am I supposed to do?" Griffin challenged. "Nothing? While they banish me to Jail For Kids? While they threaten me with juvie and a criminal record? While I pay for somebody else's crime?"

"What we expect you to do," his mother said sternly, "is trust your parents to look out for your interests. And trust our lawyer to do the right thing for you. Mostly, we expect you to obey the judge and stay out of trouble until this horrible ordeal is behind us."

That was the most devastating blow of all. Slammed with house arrest, unable to prove his innocence, Griffin was at the mercy of the justice system. And everybody knew that the justice system didn't always work. There were guiltless people rotting in prison, and even on death row, because they'd been framed, just like him.

The Man With The Plan believed in planning, but mostly he believed in action. To stand idle while his entire future went down the drain was the ultimate torture for a guy like Griffin Bing.

The cafeteria at Cedarville Middle School was a crowded, boisterous place. At one corner table, however, the tone could not have been more subdued. All eyes were on Ben Slovak as he made his way from the food line to join them.

"Well?" Pitch prompted. "Did you see him?"

"If you could call it that," Ben replied tragically. "I was down on the corner and I waved at him when he came out to catch the bus to Jail For Kids."

"You didn't even talk to him?" Melissa barely whispered.

"Just on the phone over the weekend. I'm supposed to stay away from him. My mother read Celia White's new column and hit the roof."

"Yeah, did you see that?" Logan breathed. "It's a good thing she can't print kids' names, because she knew we were all there, helping Griffin. That kind of bad press could ruin my acting career."

"Would you stop thinking about yourself for once?" snapped Savannah scornfully. "Think about Griffin. House arrest! Just looking at my Luthor, tied up in our yard, reminds me of how Griffin must feel. If he's half as depressed as poor Luthor —"

"Depression is the least of his worries," Pitch put in. "He's in major, major trouble. He's going to take the fall for this, and we all know he doesn't have that ring. Egan does."

Ben nodded. "There are good principals and bad principals, but Dr. Evil is in a class by himself. How could anybody do this to a kid?"

Pitch was bitter. "We can't let him get away with this."

"I don't care what he gets away with," Ben said unhappily. "I just want Griffin back."

Melissa's voice was quiet, but as usual, her words cut straight to the heart of the matter. "If Griffin was here, he wouldn't be complaining about how unfair it is. He'd be thinking of a way to fix it."

Helpless glances were traded up and down the table. It seemed that the one team member who would know what to do was the one who was missing in action.

11

There were no lockers at Jail For Kids. The JFK faculty didn't think it was a good idea to provide their troubled students with ready-made hiding places. As a result, everyone carried around a heavy knapsack of books and possessions, creating traffic jams in the halls and countless sore backs.

One of Sheldon Brickhaus's favorite "greetings" was to come up behind Griffin and pull on his pack so hard that the straps cut off the circulation to his lungs. It always got a panicked reaction from Griffin, punctuated by a cry of shock and terrified wheezing.

Today, however, it passed almost unnoticed, which Shank found surprising and unsatisfying.

"What's up with you, Justice? You're a shadow of your former self."

"Leave me alone," Griffin grumbled, too wrapped up in his own problems to worry about what Shank might do to him. Things were so awful that any change counted as an improvement, even being pounded into hamburger by his JFK classmate.

Shank was not the type to be driven off. "Okay, give it up. What's wrong?"

"You've got to be kidding me." Griffin was bitter. "Look around you! Maybe you think you belong in this dump; I don't."

The short, powerfully built boy was skeptical. "Yeah, but you didn't belong here last week, either, and you weren't like this. Something happened over the weekend. What?"

Even through his deep funk, Griffin couldn't help noticing that Sheldon Brickhaus was a lot sharper than the mindless sawed-off muscle-headed bully that he chose to present to the world.

Still, Griffin was in no mood to bare his soul to a Hummer with size-fourteen construction boots. "What do you care?" he muttered.

"What are you talking about? We're *friends*!"

Search as he might, Griffin could find no insincerity in Shank's concrete features. This serial torturer actually considered himself a friend! Griffin could only imagine how he treated his enemies.

Surviving the rest of the school day brought no relief. He peered bleakly through the flyspecked bus window at a town he barely recognized. Cedarville, where he'd lived his whole life, seemed as alien as the surface of Mars.

Except for a thirty-second conversation with Ben on Saturday, he'd had no contact with his friends since the courthouse debacle. Oh, yeah, and Ben waving from a distance this morning. It was better than nothing, he guessed, but his friend sure hadn't tried to get any closer. Were Griffin's friends abandoning him? He couldn't blame them if they were. He certainly didn't want them to share his fate, but it hurt to be facing this alone.

His mother was waiting at the bus stop. Another humiliation. Twelve years old, and Mommy had to walk him the forty feet to his front door, thanks to Judge Koretsky. Mom couldn't take the chance that her loser son might dawdle on the way home while under house arrest. Also, it might have been just his imagination, but he had been noticing a lot more patrol cars cruising down their quiet little street.

He caught a smirk from behind the beard of the six-foot-four high schooler. A few of the more prominent lowlifes pounded at the bus windows. Now Griffin would be branded as the mama's boy of JFK. *Perfect*, Griffin thought, *spread it around. Why should Shank have all the fun?*

The effort of maintaining a smile was practically breaking Mom's face. "How was school, dear?" she asked.

"You're kidding, right?"

She sighed. "Humor me, Griffin. I know it's a rough time, but we still have to try to live our lives."

As he trudged upstairs and faced the prospect of being shut in until bus time tomorrow, it didn't feel like he was living his own life or anybody else's.

Griffin Bing had no life.

The boredom set in almost immediately. He never thought he'd miss homework, but he could have used a little now, just to pass the time. There wasn't any homework at JFK — probably because no one would do it.

He was almost asleep from the sheer inactivity when there was a scratching and scrabbling at his window. He pulled the curtain aside and jumped back in shock.

A hairy, scrunched-up monkey face grinned in at him — Cleopatra, Savannah's pet capuchin.

He pulled up the sash. "Cleo, go home! Savannah's probably calling the FBI right now! Go on, beat it!"

The monkey stayed, hanging on to the shutter by her tail. That was when Griffin noticed the note card stuffed under her collar. He reached out and drew her into the room. A second later, the message was in his trembling fingers.

COME TO THE BASEMENT

With Cleopatra tucked under his arm like a football, he took the steps three at a time, careful to shield his passenger as he passed by the front hall, where Mom might spot him. He raced down the next flight and jumped to the cement floor. There, pressed against a high casement, was another face, this one human. Ben.

Griffin stood on a chair and opened the window. They all poured in — Ben first, followed by Savannah, Pitch, Logan, and Melissa.

"Man, am I ever glad to see you guys!" Griffin exclaimed. "What are you doing here?"

"We came to show you something," Pitch replied.

"Show me what?"

"This." Ben held out a sheet of paper, neatly folded in half.

Griffin was completely bewildered. "What is it?"

Savannah was impatient. "What do you think it is? How many times have you told us the only way to get anything accomplished is to have a plan?"

Slowly, Griffin unfolded the page and caught a glimpse of the heading at the top:

OPERATION STAKEOUT

He stared at the words. "You guys made a *plan*? For *me*?"

"So help me, Griffin," Pitch warned, "if you're going to cry, I'm out of here!"

"No — it's just — I didn't think — I can't believe —"

The emotion was almost overwhelming. Here he was, The Man With The Plan, backed into a corner where no plan was possible. And along came his five best friends in the world with this precious page. Even if their plan turned out to be idiotic and useless, it was still the greatest gift he would ever receive.

OBJECTIVE: To PROVE Dr. Evil stole the Super Bowl ring.

METHOD: Intense SURVEILLANCE of Egan home.

BASE OF OPERATIONS: Drysdales' ATTIC. Window has unobstructed view of TARGET RESIDENCE.

THE TEAM:
PITCH BENSON, climber
Mission: Placing cameras and listening devices in trees and on roof.
MELISSA DUKAKIS, technology
Mission: Computer monitoring of electronic surveillance.
BEN SLOVAK, spy
Mission: Eavesdropping from small hiding places.
LOGAN KELLERMAN, actor
Mission: Using theatrical skill to befriend Dr. Evil's daughter.
SAVANNAH DRYSDALE, command center manager
Mission: Running base of operations and keeping parents out.

LUTHOR, distraction specialist
Mission: Providing audio cover (barking).

This plan is dedicated to our friend Griffin Bing,
who never let us down.

"What do you think?" Ben asked anxiously.

"A stakeout!" Griffin's eyes were alight with excitement. "It's so simple that it's brilliant! We know he's got the ring. All we have to do is watch him. He's bound to make a mistake. I just wish I could be there with you."

Melissa stepped forward. "Show me your computer. I can stream the whole stakeout to you live. You'll see what we see."

"That's awesome!" Griffin crowed. "You only left one thing out — when?"

Savannah cradled Cleopatra lovingly. "No time like the present. My parents are going out to dinner. We set up tonight."

12

The command center was dusty and unfinished, with a plywood floor and exposed beams on the walls. The attic was jam-packed with boxes, luggage, and an amazing amount of sporting equipment — tents, kayaks, Coleman stoves. The Drysdales had been big-time campers before their daughter's growing collection of animals kept them tethered to home for all but the occasional overnight.

The low ceiling slanted downward with the A-line of the roof, meeting the baseboard everywhere except at a single dormer window. It looked out over the street and — more important — the Egan home.

Ben crouched on the floor, wrapping duct tape around the broken leg of a camera tripod. The long telephoto lens loomed over him, peering out the dormer. It was focused on the principal's living room window, waiting to capture a glimpse of the stolen Super Bowl ring for Judge Koretsky.

Suddenly, he felt hot breath on the back of his neck. He looked up to find himself staring into Luthor's gaping mouth from point-blank range.

With a wheeze, he leaped to his feet. *Wham!* His head slammed into the sloping ceiling with such force that Ferret Face popped out of his shirt. The small weasel-like creature was already running when he hit the floor. He skittered across the plywood and disappeared up the leg of Logan's jeans.

"Hey!" Logan began to shake his leg wildly until the ferret abandoned his pants and scrambled back to Ben.

Pitch grinned. "I thought you were just an actor. I didn't know you could dance, too."

"Big joke." Logan was insulted. "I'm preparing for a complex and challenging role."

"What's so challenging?" asked Savannah. "All you have to do is make friends with Egan's daughter to see if you can find out where her dad stashed the ring."

"But I'm *not* friends with Egan's daughter," Logan lectured. "I have to get in character. It takes concentration — which you can't do when you're being attacked by a wild animal!" He glowered at the ferret in Ben's hands.

"Speaking of wild animals" — Pitch turned to Savannah — "how's your little rodent problem? I don't do rats."

"Oh, that's all over — I hope," Savannah assured her. "We haven't seen him in a while. Although he could pop back up at any time. Luthor's on the lookout!"

"Hang on, you guys —" Melissa was pounding the keyboard of one of the three networked laptops that were the brains of Operation Stakeout. "Just a few more seconds . . . there!" She clicked the mouse, and Griffin's face appeared on the center screen.

There was applause in the attic.

Melissa did not join the celebration. Where computers were concerned, she was all business. "Are you with us?"

"I can see you guys," Griffin's tinny voice came through the speaker, "but how will I be able to check out what's going on at Dr. Evil's place?"

"I'll set up a split screen so you can follow the remote cameras once they're online," Melissa assured him.

"I'd give anything to be there with you guys," Griffin said wanly.

"You might want to rethink that," advised Ben as a droplet of dog drool landed on his sneaker.

Pitch fidgeted with the nervous impatience of someone with a job to do. "What are we waiting for? It's dark enough. I can be up those trees, on the roof, and finished before Egan looks out his window."

"Not yet," Savannah cautioned. "I've been watching that house. Trust me, we'll know when it's time."

Ten minutes later, her strategy became clear. The front door of 44 Honeybee Street opened, and out stepped Dr. Egan, along with his wife and their two children — an eleven-year-old girl on a razor scooter and a three-year-old boy in a stroller.

"What is it?" asked Griffin over the laptop.

"Right on schedule," said Savannah with satisfaction. "The Egans take a family walk every night around now. They're gone between forty minutes and an hour. Sometimes they come back with ice cream."

Ben squinted out the window. "Anybody know the daughter? Does she go to our school?"

"I think she's a sixth grader at the elementary," Savannah replied. "Why?"

Ben looked uncomfortable. "I guess I never thought Dr. Evil could have a daughter who looks — you know — nice."

"Don't worry," Logan assured all of them. "I'll craft a character so perfect it will reveal her like an X-ray. If she knows where the ring is, so will we."

"Don't get fancy," Griffin advised from the laptop. "She may be new in town, but you're not. If you make up some cockamamy identity, somebody will come along and call you by your real name. And then you're busted."

Pitch grabbed the knapsack that held the surveillance equipment. "The coast is clear." She reached for Ben's arm. "We're on."

As they exited the house and scampered across the street, Ben felt the familiar pounding in his ears. Another operation. Even now, the word stuck in his throat. He was fairly sure normal people didn't get mixed up in anything that had to be called Operation _____. But then he thought of Griffin and hurried along.

At the Egans' property line, he and Pitch separated. Pitch melted into the boughs of a lush sycamore, and Ben headed for the lookout spot — the wood box on the front porch.

At the sound of his own footsteps on the plank deck, a chill ran along his spine. He was a scant five feet from Dr. Evil's front door. If ever a place counted as behind enemy lines, this had to be it.

He slipped under the hinged lid and into the woodpile. A cricket chirped close enough to his ear to stop his heart.

Bugs! There are bugs in here!

In a flash, Ferret Face was out and munching on an earwig.

Go, little buddy! Eat 'em all!

He stuck a wood chip under the lid, which gave him a view of the front yard and the street in both directions. Peering straight up, he caught sight of Pitch, high in the tree, affixing the first wireless webcam to a branch.

"First camera's in place," he murmured into his walkie-talkie.

"Roger that," came Savannah's voice. "How's Pitch?"

He watched her scramble back down the first trunk with the ease of a squirrel. Her high-flying confidence was a mystery to Ben. "Nuts," he said honestly. "She's heading up the second tree. . . ."

It was the last thing Ben remembered for several minutes.

*   *   *

Pitch wrapped the Velcro strap around the second webcam, setting it firmly in place pointed at an upstairs window.

Hanging on to the tree, she spoke into the walkie-talkie clipped to the front of her shirt. "Number two in place. Check it."

"Point it down slightly," came Melissa's instructions.

Pitch tapped at the tiny device.

"Perfect," Melissa approved.

"Great. I'll place the microphone and then I'm out of here." That meant she had to get to the roof.

She found a sturdy limb that reached toward the house and crept along it as far as she dared. Then, in a remarkable display of balance, she transferred herself onto the dark green shingles. The roof was sloped, but she stepped lightly, with sure feet, and made her way to the chimney.

From the backpack, she took the final surveillance device Melissa had provided — a wireless microphone on a long, thin rope. She tied the end of the tether to the steel mesh of the chimney cap and lowered the unit down the shaft. If Melissa's calculations were right — and the shy girl was never wrong — the microphone should hang in the fireplace, just out of sight. From there, it would pick up most of what was being said in the entire house.

Her face twisted. *Bad enough we have to listen to the guy all day in school; now we have to hear him singing in the shower!*

But of course it was worth it — for Griffin.

For the first time, she noticed it was raining a little — tiny cold drops. It would be a good idea to get off this roof before the shingles became wet and slippery. Gingerly, she started toward the eaves.

And froze.

There, hurrying up the street, were the Egans, coming home early because of the rain. And not a peep of warning from Ben Slovak, the lookout.

She was trapped on the roof!

13

Pitch ducked back behind the chimney. "Ben!" she hissed into the walkie-talkie. A soft snore was her reply. "Ferret Face, what are you doing? Your man's sleeping on the job!"

In the wood box, Ben awoke with a start. "What? What?"

"Shhh, you idiot! Egan's coming up the front walk!"

Ben looked around, desperately trying to reacquire his bearings. Beside him, Ferret Face was chasing a grasshopper around a big log. No wonder he'd fallen asleep, with the animal bug-hunting instead of keeping him awake. He grabbed the ferret and stuck him back inside his shirt.

His mind raced. *Should I make a run for it?*

The first footfall hit the porch.

Too late!

There wasn't even time to remove the chip propping open the wood box. If Dr. Evil looked over and wondered why the lid was slightly ajar . . .

Ben hugged his ferret to his chest and prayed for invisibility.

The daughter passed by — blond hair, turned-up nose.

She has freckles — you can't see them from a distance. . . .

"Let's go, Lindsay," came the mother's voice. "Leave your scooter where it won't get wet."

Her name is Lindsay. . . .

A split second later, all rational thought was paralyzed. The narrow strip that was his field of vision was filled with Dr. Evil. The principal passed so close that Ben could practically count the man's nose hairs.

Don't see me. . . . Don't see me. . . . Don't see me. . . .

Ben hunkered down, not even daring to breathe. The next thing he heard was the front door closing. The family was gone from the porch.

In the command center in Savannah's attic, Melissa clicked her mouse, and the voices of the Egans came through one of the laptops.

"Pitch, you did it!" Savannah breathed into her walkie-talkie. "The fireplace mike is getting everything!"

"Never mind that!" rasped Ben from his hiding place. "When can we get out of here?"

"I'm not hanging around," Pitch said with conviction.

But as she started for the eaves, the microphone picked up Mrs. Egan's worried exclamation: "What's that noise? It sounds like an animal on the roof!"

"Pitch — freeze!" ordered Savannah.

"Probably just a twig falling down," the principal assured his wife. "I think the wind was picking up."

"It sounded like footsteps," she protested.

"I'll get a flashlight."

The stakeout team was prepared. "Get ready for audio cover," Savannah said into the walkie-talkie. Logan popped the window, and she guided Luthor's massive head out into the night. "Okay, sweetie, let her rip."

A 747 could not have created more noise. Luthor's thundering bark filled the neighborhood, rattling windows and sending smaller pets scurrying.

Pitch came off the roof, flew down the tree trunk, and hit the ground running. At that, she was several steps behind Ben, who exploded out of the wood box as if propelled by a catapult. They flashed across the street and flew up the Drysdales' stairs to the attic.

Savannah was just quieting Luthor. "Nice work, you guys."

"You wouldn't have thought it was nice if it happened to you!" panted Ben.

Pitch nodded vigorously, too breathless to comment.

"Don't worry, it's all going perfectly," came Griffin's voice through the laptop. "What next?"

"We keep watch," Savannah replied.

And they did — through little Anthony's bath time, through Lindsay's French horn practice, and through an hour-long documentary on cheese making on the Discovery Channel.

"This is really boring," Logan complained. "When are they going to take out the ring?"

That, they were coming to realize, was the whole problem with stakeouts. Setting up the surveillance was the easy part. The real challenge was waiting for something important to happen.

And there was no guarantee that it ever would.

14

Gym class at the JFK Alternative Education Center consisted of only one activity — dodgeball. Not once had Griffin made it through an entire day without being involved in at least one match.

"They can't trust us with sticks or bats," was Sheldon Brickhaus's explanation. "But they still want us to work out our aggression. So they buy a bunch of floppy rubber balls from Babies"R"Us and turn us loose on the floor."

Shank had reason to know. He was the greatest dodgeball player in the history of the sport. He could take a ball designed for a toddler and turn it into a weapon of mass destruction. It wasn't enough for him to hit you with the ball. He had an eye for finding you unbalanced or hyperextended. Then he'd nail you in the ear, or the side of the knee, or the neck with such surgical precision that it would knock you flat. Even the high schoolers with criminal records were afraid of him on the dodgeball court.

As Shank's "friend," Griffin was targeted without mercy. The only escape was to hurl himself in front of someone else's normal throw in order to be eliminated from the game.

Today, though, Griffin's mind was so awhirl with the details of Operation Stakeout that there was no room for survival skills. Soon, he found himself standing like a deer in headlights as the dodgeball master lined him up for the kill.

"Say your prayers, Justice! This one's going down your throat!"

Even then, with the guided missile seconds away, Griffin was miles from the gym, in the Drysdales' attic, where Melissa's surveillance gear was on automatic, filming and recording the Egan house. Was there any chance of catching a glimpse of the ring while Dr. Evil was at school all day? Not likely. For all Griffin knew, Mrs. Egan worked, too, and they were recording eight hours of nothing.

When the shot came, it wasn't the hammer blow designed to lay him out. Shank bounced the ball softly off his shoulder. Then, in an eerily quiet voice, he said, "You're hit. Get out of my face."

Griffin was grateful to leave the court and give Operation Stakeout his full attention. Not that he could ever be anything more than a spectator watching the whole thing from his room.

He wasn't sure what was worse — house arrest, or missing out on a plan. Either way, it was horrible to be powerless to affect your own fate.

He struggled to stay positive. His friends had come up with a great plan, every bit as good as any idea of his. But, face it, a stakeout was a passive thing. You couldn't go and get the truth; it had to come to you. What if it never did?

An *oof* of pain indicated that the game had ended. It was time to head to the locker room to endure Shank's other athletic talent — towel snapping. But when the burly boy sat down beside Griffin on the bench, he was unarmed.

"You know, Justice, you really get on my nerves."

Griffin was amazed. "What did *I* do?"

"Is my life such a party that I can pass up a chance to put a dodgeball through your skull? I don't think so."

"So who's stopping you?" Griffin asked.

"You are! You're so — *nice*! It takes the fun out of everything!"

"Then ignore me," Griffin shot back.

"I can't. This place is full of the worst lowlifes in town, and I survive being lower than the lot of them. The whole thing stinks, but it all makes sense — except you."

Why was Sheldon Brickhaus the only person who understood that Griffin didn't belong at Jail For Kids? Why couldn't the police see that? Why couldn't Judge Koretsky?

Then again, if the team couldn't come up with that Super Bowl ring, the judge would sentence him to someplace a whole lot worse.

Honeybee Street was perfect for riding a scooter — freshly repaved, with a gentle slope.

Eleven-year-old Lindsay Egan came freewheeling along the blacktop, wind rustling the long, fair hair that trailed out of her helmet. She'd worked hard on her balance, and it showed.

A second scooter rider was coming from the opposite direction, struggling to get his vehicle up the incline. As Lindsay flashed by, Logan said, "Hi!"

It was only one syllable, but he spoke it in the character he had developed for making friends with Lindsay. Unfortunately, she passed by too quickly to notice, and probably missed it altogether.

Undaunted, he wheeled around and launched himself after her. He was going slightly downhill now, picking up speed, hearing the wind rushing by his ears. It was better, he decided, in this direction. Gravity did most of the work, so he could devote all his energy to acting.

By this time, Lindsay had turned at the end of the block and was on her way up.

"Nice scooter!" Logan called as he passed.

"Thanks." And she was gone again.

Better, but not exactly a relationship. No way was he going to get to know her well enough to bring up the subject of the Super Bowl ring if all they did was flash past each other at twenty miles an hour.

There were moments in the career of an actor when he needed to make a bolder artistic choice. For the good of the performance, that moment had to be now.

He glanced over his shoulder to make sure she'd reached the top and was starting down again. Then he pumped at the pavement, working up a humongous head of steam. By the time he hit the curb and jumped the sidewalk, he was flying.

The bush he'd been aiming at — the one that looked so soft and cushioning — wasn't quite what he'd expected. His head slammed into hard wood, and dozens of sharp thorns ripped at his skin.

When he screamed, he didn't even have to use his acting ability. This scream was the real thing.

She was at his side in an instant. "Are you alive?"

"Maybe," he said faintly. "My head hurts and — could you get me out of this bush?"

She helped pull him free. "You're all torn up. And we need to ice the bump on your head. Come on." She began to lead him along the street.

"What about the scooters?" he protested weakly.

"We'll come back for them. I live right over there."

Logan allowed himself to be guided down the road, passing right under the attic dormer, where he knew the rest of the team was watching with great interest.

*   *   *

Ben was squinting out the window in consternation. "Why's she holding his hand?"

Savannah, who was looking through the telephoto lens of the camera, had a better view. "I think he's *bleeding*."

"Don't worry," Pitch put in sarcastically. "Good actors can bleed on cue."

"What happened to you back there?" Lindsay was asking. "One minute you were doing fine, and the next you were gone!"

"I don't remember," said Logan. "But it seems to me they could have found a better place to put a bush."

She laughed. "I'm Lindsay."

"Logan. You're new in town, right?"

"We just moved here — from upstate. Watch out for the flower beds," she added as they made their way onto the Egans' front walk. "I'm putting in bulbs for the spring — tulips, daffodils, hyacinths. I'm really into spring flowers."

"Oh, yeah — me, too," said Logan, making a mental note to check out the subject on Wikipedia. An actor had to do research to support a role.

She let them in the front door and pointed him in the direction of the bathroom. "You can wash up in there. I'll get an ice pack for that bruise. It's turning black and blue."

"Thanks." Logan was pleased with himself. Now *this* was what acting could do. All that climbing around in trees and on the roof, all that technology, and what did they have? A murky view of a couple of windows, and sounds from the TV and toilets flushing. But a little bit of acting, and here he was in the lion's den. Wouldn't it be something if he found the ring himself, before the stakeout even got going? He'd be a hero!

His mind wrapped itself around that possibility. Would it be better to swipe the ring right away? Or maybe he should leave it here and come back with the cops? That would prove Dr. Evil took it. . . .

He splashed a little water on his face. The cuts still stung, but that was a small price to pay to ace a role. When he emerged, feeling much better, Lindsay beckoned him into the kitchen.

"I couldn't find an ice pack, but these frozen lima beans should do the trick."

There, holding a bag of frozen vegetables against his forehead, Logan made an exciting discovery. A blue velvet jewelry box sat on the counter next to the toaster oven.

The ring? There was only one way to find out. He had to get a look inside that box. But how could he do that with Lindsay standing right there? He was mentally searching his bag of theatrical tricks when a car door slammed outside.

A moment later, Dr. Evil was standing in the front hall.

15

Logan panicked like no actor ever should. He covered his face with the lima bean package, stammered, "I gotta go!" and blasted right past the astonished principal and out the door.

Lindsay's "But it's just my dad . . ." trailed off.

Logan had left the building.

"Real smooth, Kellerman," Pitch said sometime later in the stakeout command center. "Especially the lima beans. You might get nominated for Best Makeup — first actor to break the Vegetable Barrier."

"Okay, so I lost it," Logan admitted sheepishly. "I saw Egan and I pictured myself rotting in Jail For Kids with the dregs of society."

"Thanks a lot," came Griffin's voice over the laptop.

Logan sat down on a box of old *National Geographic*s and tried to catch his breath. Unwilling to lead the principal across the street to the Drysdales', he had reclaimed his scooter and ridden around for forty-five minutes, waiting for the coast to clear. The pain from salty sweat in his many cuts had been almost too much to bear. But he'd fought through his suffering in order to return to the command center and deliver his ultra-important news.

"Guys — I think I know where the ring is!"

"Where?" chorused everyone, including Griffin over the speaker.

"There's a jewelry box on the kitchen counter. I couldn't get a look inside. Egan showed up right after I spotted it."

Ben was confused. "Who keeps jewelry in the kitchen?"

"Nobody," Griffin concluded. "Not unless you're waiting to take it out somewhere."

"He's selling it!" Pitch concluded.

"Or maybe he's going to have it melted down for the gold and the diamonds," Savannah added anxiously.

Griffin was alarmed. "We can't let him do that! Then we'd never be able to prove that it used to be Art Blankenship's ring!"

"I can move one of the webcams," Pitch suggested. "Maybe there's an angle that looks in the kitchen window."

"It still wouldn't be clear enough," Griffin decided. "We need to know for sure. Logan, can you get back in the house?"

"No problem," Logan said confidently. "I think that girl Lindsay kind of likes me."

"I don't know if that's such a good idea," Ben said quickly. "You made a pretty big idiot of yourself back there. And besides, you ripped off their lima beans."

Logan frowned at him. "An actor learns to improvise and cover little mistakes. As for the lima beans, I'll just bring them back."

"I don't think so," Melissa put in quietly.

All eyes followed her pointing finger to the plywood floor, where Luthor's huge snout was buried in the ripped-open freezer bag.

Savannah leaped forward, grabbed the big dog's collar, and yanked the Doberman away from his snack. "Luthor — you know legumes give you gas!"

"We've got to move fast," Griffin urged the

team. "Tomorrow after school. Logan, can you be ready?"

"I have play rehearsal tonight," Logan replied. "And I need to do some research on flowers so I can help Lindsay plant her bulbs. That's my dramatic opportunity."

"Don't worry. Ben will do the research for you."

"No way!" Ben exploded. "Why do I have to help him hit on Lindsay?"

"I'm not hitting on her," Logan protested. "I just need a reason to be over there helping her plant. Then I'll ask to use the bathroom and look inside the jewelry box."

"I'll e-mail it to you tonight," Ben said. "But you'd better use it just for the meeting."

At that moment, the buildup of lima beans in Luthor's system had its dreaded effect.

The stakeout was quickly adjourned.

16

The next day, Logan snuck out of the science lab a few minutes before the end of last period and rushed to his locker. He stowed his books and paused to regard himself in the mirror on the inside of the door — the one that showed his reflection in an oval of stars. His many cuts and scratches were more pronounced than ever, thanks to the dark scabs. And the lump on his forehead was a deep purple. Certainly not his best look, but an interesting one. Actors had to make do with the raw materials available.

At rehearsal last night, Mrs. Arturo, the director of *Hail Caesar*, had gasped at the sight of him. Luckily, she had been a makeup artist during her days on Broadway. No skin blemish, she'd explained, was so severe that it could not be erased with the right powder. Mom, on the other hand, had never worked in drama. Why did these nontheatrical people have to be so emotional?

He locked up and headed for the stairwell. Halfway down, he passed the principal.

Dr. Egan did a double take. "Logan, what happened to your face?"

"Uh — mosquito bites," Logan replied. "I guess I scratched them in my sleep."

The principal cast him a crooked smile. "I think you'd better apply some more lima beans when you get home."

Logan could not get out of the school quickly enough. So Dr. Evil had guessed that his had been the face behind the frozen vegetables. And now Logan was heading back to the very same house for round two.

But the show must go on. As long as Griffin was still banished to Jail For Kids, the operation was all that mattered.

Logan's first stop, though, was Cedarville Elementary. Funny — up until this year, he and his friends had all attended this school. How could it have gotten so dinky in just a few months?

The dismissal bell rang, and he sat on a rock by the sixth-grade wing. Soon the school yard was filled with elementary kids. But Logan only had eyes for one.

"Lindsay — hi!"

She was beaming as she joined him. "Logan — what are you doing here?"

"I was in the neighborhood."

She laughed. "Isn't this *your* neighborhood, too?"

"I remembered you were going to be planting bulbs today. I figured I could give you a hand. I've got a lot of experience." At least, he had enough crib notes from Ben to fake it. Despite his complaining, the small, slight boy had come through with four pages of information on spring planting last night.

Her smile got even brighter. "Great!" As they headed for Honeybee Street, she made a confession. "You know, my dad kind of warned me to stay away from you. He said, 'If it's the Logan I think it is, he's part of that gang Celia White's always writing about.'"

Uh-oh. This kind of negative advance buzz could undermine a performance.

"Well — uh — what do *you* think?"

"I'm with you, aren't I? I respect my dad, but he doesn't pick my friends for me."

At the Egan house, Lindsay opened the door,

tossed her bag in the front hall, and called, "Mom — I'm going to do some planting."

She stepped into the garage and emerged with two hand spades and a basket of bulbs. In a few minutes, they were side by side on their knees, digging holes and planting daffodils for next spring.

"I hope you got some of the blue ones," Logan commented as he shoveled. "They're the rarest."

She looked at him oddly. "All daffodils are yellow."

"Like I said, the rarest," Logan blustered. He must have read that part of the research wrong. "I know the bulbs are considered a delicacy in Canada," he ventured in an attempt to recover.

"No, they're not. They're poison." She leaned over his shoulder. "What are you doing — digging a tunnel to China?"

"But — but the bulbs have to be planted at least two feet deep."

"Logan!" she exclaimed. "Where did you learn about gardening? Six inches is plenty."

"But — but —" He stood up, totally flustered. What was going on? Why had Ben fed him wrong information? How could an actor play his part when the script was full of mistakes? "I have to go to the bathroom!" he blurted, and ran into the house. This performance was ruined. All he could do was get a look inside the jewelry box and get out of there. It wouldn't win any Oscars, but at least the job would be done.

He burst through the door and ran into the kitchen.

"Oh — hello. I'm Lindsay's mother."

Oh, no! Mrs. Evil!

Logan fastened his eyes hungrily on the blue velvet box, so close, yet so far away. "Uh — hi."

"You must be the lima bean boy. Logan, is it? I'll bet your mother had something to say about what happened to your face."

Utter, paralyzing stage fright. He wasn't sure he could live with the humiliation. Not only was he totally blowing this, but, up in Savannah's attic, all his friends could hear every word he wasn't saying through the chimney mike.

He tried to mumble, "Nice meeting you," but it came out more like "Mice neeting goo." His face must have been bright red as he finally escaped, because, when he got out to Lindsay, she made an extra effort to be kind.

"Don't feel bad, Logan. I'll teach you everything you need to know about gardening." She gave his hand a squeeze. "I'll be right back." And she scampered across the porch and into the house.

The instant the door closed behind her, the lid of the wood box flew open, and out vaulted Ben Slovak, a compact whirlwind of fury.

"You're busted, Kellerman!"

Logan could not have been more astonished if a giant squid tentacle had reached out of there and grabbed him. "Why aren't you in the command center? Are you spying on me?"

"Oh, horror!" Ben sneered. "We can't have any spying — besides the webcams in the trees, the microphone in the chimney, and the telephoto lens across the street!"

"Get out of here!" Logan hissed. "She could be back any minute!"

"You'd like that, wouldn't you?" Ben seethed. "Then you'd have her all to yourself — you and your shovels and your bulbs!"

"It's not like that! I'm acting!"

"Yeah — acting like a moron!"

"At least I'm doing my job!" Logan defended himself. "That's more than I can say for you — feeding me all those bogus facts! I could have taken a bite out of one of those bulbs and be dead right now!"

All at once, both boys realized that their argument was being drowned out by a loud roaring bark.

"Luthor!" wheezed Ben.

"The signal!" added Logan.

And that could mean only one thing. Dr. Egan's car had been spotted from the attic.

In a heartbeat, the anger between them was transformed into pure speed. They dashed across the street, diving behind the Drysdales' hedge a split second before the principal's Hyundai whispered past. Then they blasted in through the door, startling Savannah's mother, who was sorting through a pantry filled with a dozen different kinds of animal feed.

"Oh, hi, boys —"

But they were already halfway up the stairs en route to the attic.

Pitch greeted them, close to hysterics. "What was *that* supposed to be? Are you both crazy? Ben, what were you doing in the wood box?"

"I had to stop Romeo here from letting his love for Lindsay get in the way of the operation!"

Logan was furious. "For the twentieth time, I don't even like her! Maybe *you're* the one who likes her!"

That was the last straw for Ben. He hurled

himself at Logan, sending the larger boy stagger-
ing backward into the camera tripod. It went down
with a crash, punctuated by breaking glass — the
telephoto lens.

Ferret Face darted out of Ben's shirt and took
cover up a support beam as Ben kept a choke hold
on Logan and would not let go.

"It — was — acting!" Logan insisted, slamming
Ben against the table that held the three laptops.
Only Melissa's frantic efforts kept the whole setup
from hitting the floor.

"What's going on over there?" Griffin's voice
echoed throughout the attic. "Has everybody
gone nuts?"

Pitch and Savannah each grabbed a combatant,
but they could not manage to pull Ben and Logan
apart.

"Cut it out, you guys!" Savannah begged. "My
mom's home!"

And then a new voice sounded in the command
center. It came through the speaker of the third
laptop, the one that monitored the chimney mike.
Instant silence fell in the attic. It was the voice of
Dr. Evil:

"Okay, I'll be back soon. I'm going to swing by
the jewelers and drop this off."

17

The five team members squeezed into the dormer window. They watched breathlessly as their principal, the blue velvet box in his hand, left the house and climbed into his car. He backed out of the driveway and headed down the street, making a left turn off Honeybee toward town.

"What's happening?" Griffin demanded in a half-demented rasp.

"This is it, Griffin!" Ben exclaimed, wild with excitement. "He's got the box and he's heading for the jewelry store!"

"Follow him!" Griffin ordered.

"He's in a car!" Pitch protested.

"There's only one jeweler in Cedarville," Griffin reasoned. "Konrad's, on Main Street. We've got to take a picture of the ring while Dr. Evil's holding it!"

As they raced for the attic stairs, Ben snatched Ferret Face down off the beam and stuffed him under his shirt. Savannah threw open the door. There stood her mother, who had come up to investigate the commotion. Her eyes bulged at the sight of the computer screens with their detailed views of the Egan home.

"Savannah Marie Drysdale, you'd better have an explanation for all this!"

"I do — later!"

And then Mrs. Drysdale was alone with Luthor, amid the ruins of Operation Stakeout.

Up in his room, Griffin stared at his computer monitor, which showed a bewildered Lindsay standing by her flower bed, trying to discover what had happened to her planting partner. She even looked inside the wood box, because the lid was open. The split-screen image showed the command center in Savannah's attic was empty.

"Guys?" Griffin said into the microphone. "Is anybody still there?"

"Who is that?" came the sharp voice of Mrs. Drysdale. Her bewildered face tilted into his monitor.

Griffin was out of his room and down the stairs before conscious thought kicked in.

House arrest! I can't go!

He was not allowed out that door, except to go to Jail For Kids. That wasn't just a rule, like no running in the hall. It was *law*, imposed by a real judge, and enforced by the police department!

It almost tore him in two. Half a mile away, at Konrad's Jewelry Designs, the most important event of his life was about to take place. And he couldn't be there.

Not that he didn't trust his friends. But there were so many things that could go wrong. They could arrive too late and miss the moment when the ring was revealed. Or too early — and be spotted. Then Dr. Evil would keep the ring underground.

They could take a bad picture that was worthless as evidence. Or forget the camera altogether in the rush to get to the store. And if today didn't pan out, there'd be no second chances. The stakeout was in shambles; the command center compromised; and the principal would know they were on to him.

Griffin set his jaw. His friends were great — the best. But a successful plan required a master planner. And none of them was that.

I have to be there!

Throwing on a jacket, he did a quick accounting of the whereabouts of his parents, who would definitely not be cool about this. Mom was in the backyard, cleaning out her greenhouse for the winter. And Dad was in the garage, working on the Vole-B-Gone.

Uh-oh. His bike was in the garage. No way could he get it without Dad seeing him. He opened the closet and pulled on his old Rollerblades. A little tight, but sore feet were the least of his worries right now.

He pocketed his father's cell phone, which had a camera, and slipped out the door, careful not to slam it. If Mom or Dad happened to check on him and find him gone, payback would be a monster. In the end, though, everything would be okay — with his parents, the judge, even with the school — once the ring had been recovered. He couldn't wait to see their faces when he was proven innocent. And Celia White would have to print a huge apology in her stupid column.

He almost fell down the front steps, but managed to save himself and hit the road at top speed. Long, powerful strides ate up the distance downtown.

A police cruiser went by as Griffin made the turn onto Main Street. Blind panic coursed through him, but he did his best not to look like a fugitive. The car drove on. The officer did not recognize him.

He could see the gold awning in front of Konrad's, two blocks away.

A gray Hyundai Sonata wheeled onto Main from a side street. Dr. Evil! Had Griffin gone through all this only to arrive too late?

He bore down, pouring every ounce of strength in his body into the pumping of his legs. His muscles burned and so did the breath in his throat. Oh, no! The principal was right in front of the store. . . .

Wait — no place to park! Hooray! The Hyundai continued down the block and began to reverse into a spot past the store.

Griffin was almost there. One more street before the gold awning . . .

The bicycle appeared out of nowhere, directly in his path. He reached out and grabbed the rider in a desperate attempt to save them both. His momentum very nearly took them into a shattering wipeout against a brick wall. But at the last second, the biker managed to right them and bring them to a shaky stop.

"Griffin!" Savannah hissed. "You're on house arrest!"

"I won't be a few minutes from now," he whispered back. "Quick — hide!"

They ducked around the corner of the building and peeked out. The principal was having trouble parallel parking in a tight space. It gave them a moment to catch their breath.

"Where are the others?" Griffin asked urgently.

"Running."

He could already see the rest of the team pounding up the sidewalk, athletic Pitch in the lead.

A car door slammed. Dr. Egan was crossing the street toward Konrad's. Griffin bladed out to greet the runners, his finger to his lips. At this sensitive moment, even heavy breathing could be enough to give them away.

Although the newcomers were surprised to see him, nobody said a word. Ben and Logan, sweaty and bruised, glared at each other. But the operation came first.

The jingling sound told them that the principal had entered Konrad's Jewelry Designs. They crept around the corner and approached the store gingerly, keeping low. Slowly — agonizingly slowly — Griffin raised himself to peer in the window.

Dr. Egan was the only customer. The jewelry box, still closed, sat on the glass showcase. The principal released the catch and opened the lid.

"Now!" breathed Griffin. He threw the door wide and rolled inside, the team at his heels.

Dr. Egan looked up, startled. He spied Griffin first. "You!"

Like a gunfighter at the O.K. Corral, Griffin whipped out the cell phone, framed a view of his principal standing over the open box, and tore off six quick shots.

Cameras flashed, team members jockeyed for the best vantage point. If anyone had ever been caught in the act, it was Dr. Egan.

At the same instant, all six noticed the contents of the jewelry box. It was an antique gold brooch with one missing drop pearl.

"That's not a Super Bowl ring!" blurted Ben.

Truer words had never been spoken.

The principal's voice dripped ice. "This is going to have consequences."

The electronic bracelet was tight and uncomfortable and squeezed his leg. Griffin was never going to get used to it — just like he was never going to get used to the idea of why he had to wear it.

"The PEMA unit sends a wireless signal to the monitoring hub we've installed in your basement," intoned Detective Sergeant Vizzini, who had just clapped the device onto Griffin's ankle.

"PEMA?" asked Mr. Bing weakly.

"Police Electronic Monitoring Anklet. I've set the range for two hundred feet, which should cover the house and most of the yard. Anything beyond that triggers an alarm at headquarters. The warning light will flash green, and you'll have ten seconds to get back in range. After that, it goes red." He looked at Griffin with expressionless eyes. "You don't want that."

The worst thing about this was that Mom couldn't look at the anklet without sobbing. "I can't believe this is happening to us! Our son is not a criminal! What would he want with Mrs. Egan's grandmother's brooch? Don't you understand that he's looking for the ring because he doesn't have it?"

"What I understand," said Vizzini, "is that he was under court-ordered house arrest, and he ignored it. Now — if you try to remove the anklet, the alarm sounds. If you try to move the hub, the alarm sounds. If you try to tamper with any of the settings, the alarm sounds. Bottom line, you're under the same house arrest. The only change is that this time you have to do it. Any questions?"

"What about school?" asked Griffin.

"You're authorized for that. Don't abuse it. JFK will be giving us updates throughout the day. And don't worry about showering. This thing's indestructible."

Before leaving, Vizzini took Mr. Bing's credit card imprint. That was the biggest insult of all. The Cedarville Police Department actually made you pay for your own PEMA monitoring — $39.95

a day, plus a security deposit. Like he was going to steal this fabulous fashion accessory.

"Well, Griffin —" His father looked like he hadn't slept in a long time. "You don't need me to tell you you're in deep trouble here."

"But I'm *innocent*," Griffin protested. "You said you believed me."

"We do," his mother whimpered softly. "But I look at that awful thing on your ankle and wonder what difference it really makes. I may be crazy, but I'd rather have you guilty and getting away with it than innocent and clapped in that leg iron."

"One thing's certain," his father went on grimly. "It definitely didn't help that you had such a reputation with the local police. So when it came to believing you, why should they?"

For Griffin, it was the ultimate blow. Throughout this whole nightmare, the one thing he'd always had going for him was the fact that his parents were on his side. They still were — sort of. But they also seemed to blame him — as if this misfortune, which he'd had no hand in, was somehow his fault. It was almost like the fact that he was innocent didn't even matter to them.

If your own mom and dad didn't support you, who would?

His friends? They were the best, loyal to the end. But this might really *be* the end. On the phone, Ben had mentioned that all five of them were having major hassles with their families over Operation Stakeout — especially Savannah, whose parents had the evidence right in their attic. At least the others weren't in trouble with the police, since Dr. Evil had never found the webcams in his trees or the microphone down his chimney. But everybody was banned from having anything to do with Griffin Bing.

The Man With The Plan was The Man With The Blame. He had the ankle bracelet to prove it.

And after all he'd suffered, all the anguish he'd caused his parents, and all the trouble his friends had gotten into for his sake, the most important question was not a single millimeter closer to being answered:

Where was Art Blankenship's Super Bowl ring?

19

It was after eight p.m., and Celia White was still at her desk.

This was nothing unusual. She always worked late. Uncovering the dark side of Cedarville and surrounding areas didn't happen during a nine-to-five shift. What was different was that she was all alone in the offices of the *Herald*. Back when she'd first started, this newsroom had bustled well into the night, filled with reporters following breaking stories and fine-tuning articles and features to perfection. Now the norm was journalists who didn't care — oh, how she missed the old days!

Well, maybe none of her colleagues took pride in their work; Celia White had a responsibility to her readers. She would stay here as long as it took to finish this latest column on youth run wild in her hometown.

But not without a little dinner.

As she left the office in search of the cheese sandwich in the glove compartment of her car, the closet door opened slowly and a shadowy figure stepped out into the room. Pitch Benson hurried to the desk, moving stealthily through the empty room. If Dr. Egan didn't have that ring — and even *that* wasn't 100 percent certain — one of the other suspects did. There was no chance for Griffin to find the real culprit now — not with an electronic bracelet on his ankle. It was up to his friends to take action on his behalf.

She began riffling through the drawers, searching. . . .

The gym bag, fully packed, sat directly under the sill.

Ben crouched outside the Vader home, peering in through the glass. No sign of Darren. Ben would never have a better chance than this.

The window sash was open about three inches — just enough space for him to reach in with his father's old beach metal detector. He passed the scanning dish over the duffel, ears alert for the beep that would indicate the presence of metal — the metal of a Super Bowl ring.

"Going to practice, Mom!" came Darren's foghorn voice from inside the house. "I'll just grab a Gatorade first."

Uh-oh. Ben withdrew the device by its long handle and ducked into the bushes, peeking in over the sill with one eye.

After a moment, Darren appeared, a half-gallon jug of Gatorade in his meaty fist. Hastily, Ben dropped out of sight and pressed himself up against the side of the house.

Darren strode over to his bag, uncorking the bottle and taking a long pull. Then, in a single motion, he threw the window wide and dumped the rest of the contents into the bushes.

The big boy smiled in satisfaction at the cry of shock that came from below.

"Hey, Slovak," he called out the window. "You stink at spying. Tell Bing he better not even think about trying to pin this rap on me. Got it?"

Drenched, muddy, and thoroughly humiliated, Ben crawled onto the Vader lawn in retreat, the metal detector dragging behind him.

"And you owe me a Gatorade!" Darren shouted after him. "You made me spill this one!"

A damp and sticky Ferret Face glowered plaintively up at Ben from his collar. A quick murmured "Sorry, pal" was all the apology Ben had time for. He had to drop the metal detector at home and meet the rest of the team at school before calisthenics.

Melissa pulled the papers from her printer and stuffed them in the computer bag that served as her backpack. Ever since the fiasco at Konrad's, she had been monitoring the e-mail of the four suspects, Celia White, Darren Vader, Tony Bartholomew, and Dr. Egan.

The meeting place was Ben's locker. This was for two reasons. First, it was close to the entrance, so they could run outside quickly when calisthenics started. And second, it was right next to Griffin's locker. That closed vented door — and the friend who was not there to open it — served as a reminder that they could not give up until they had won justice for The Man With The Plan.

Ben, Pitch, and Logan were leaning against

the beige metal row when Melissa arrived. Only Savannah could not attend. Since the discovery of the command center, her parents had been watching her every move. To leave for school an hour early would have seemed suspicious when so much heat was on. Savannah was walking on eggs.

"Celia White's a dead end," Pitch was telling the others. "There was nothing but junk in her desk." She turned to Ben. "Any luck with Vader?"

"If getting slimed with Gatorade counts, it was the luckiest day of my life," Ben replied bitterly. He squeezed the front of his sweatshirt, wringing out a trickle of yellow liquid. "His gym bag's clean, though. The metal detector didn't beep."

"I struck out with Tony Bartholomew," Logan confessed, shamefaced. "I used the Stanislavski method to portray his cousin from Arizona, but he saw right through it. I probably didn't have enough time to prepare for the role."

"Probably," Pitch agreed sarcastically. "Either that or he recognized a kid he sees around school every single day."

"I might have something on Tony," Melissa ventured, taking the papers from her bag. "He sent an e-mail asking about Super Bowl rings and how much they're worth. That could be because he's trying to sell one."

"Or he could just be pricing them since he thinks the missing one is his," Ben said with a sigh. "Face it, we're right back where we started. We can't even totally rule out Dr. Evil. Just because the ring wasn't in the box he brought to Konrad's doesn't mean he hasn't got it stashed someplace else."

Melissa parted her curtain of hair to reveal a furrowed brow. "There must be something we're missing here."

Pitch nodded slowly. "You know what always bugged me? How could a Super Bowl ring sit in the custodian's supply closet for all those years without anyone noticing it?"

"Maybe nobody recognized it for what it was," Logan suggested.

"No way," Pitch countered. "Mr. Clancy's head practically exploded when I mentioned the sixty-nine Jets, and he's in that closet, like, twenty times a day. I say we check it out."

The storage area doubled as offices for the building custodians. It was located down a half flight of steps by the back entrance. On one side of the space was the school's loading bay. On the other, the staircase continued to the furnace room in the basement.

The team approached cautiously, hugging the banister. The storeroom was off-limits to students. No one wanted to have to explain what they were doing there.

Pitch peered around the wall of the landing. No custodians. "All clear," she whispered.

They stepped out into the loading bay and saw it immediately. Mr. Clancy's work area was a symphony of blue and white. Colts posters, pennants, and bumper stickers were everywhere. The walls were plastered with photographs of great Colts players from Johnny Unitas to Peyton Manning. A Colts stadium blanket held the place of honor, draped over the custodian's desk chair.

Ferret Face stopped sucking on Ben's Gatorade-soaked collar to gaze at so much bright color.

"Whoa," said Ben. "Now we know why Mr. Clancy always wears that blue and white headband."

Logan was confused. "I wonder how he got to be such a big Colts fan. I heard he's from Maryland, not Indianapolis."

"The Colts used to play in Baltimore before moving to Indy," Pitch explained. Suddenly, her

eyes were wide. "Hold on! Nineteen sixty-nine —
Super Bowl Three! The New York Jets beat the
Baltimore Colts in the greatest upset in history!
Colts fans are still bent out of shape about it!"

"So?" All at once, Ben clued in. "Wait a minute!
You're not saying that Mr. Clancy is so mad about
a football game that he stole the ring just so he
wouldn't have to *look* at it? It was more than forty
years ago!"

"He *did* call it the worst day of his life," Logan
reminded them.

"Dr. Evil said he has the only key to the display
case," Melissa added. "But that's probably not true.
The custodians must have a copy somewhere."

Ben was unimpressed. "I don't know, you guys.
Isn't this kind of far-fetched?"

"Probably," Pitch agreed. "But at this point, far-
fetched is the best we've got."

20

The command center was just an attic again. It had taken some doing. Melissa had hauled off her three laptops and their related wiring. The card table and tripod were folded and stowed again. The telephoto lens was in the trash along with the broken glass. Also at the curb, in green garbage bags, were the many pizza boxes, fast-food containers, and drink bottles that had sustained Operation Stakeout through the long, hungry hours.

Now all that remained was to straighten up the chaos caused by Ben and Logan's wrestling match. How crazy was that? Neither of them would discuss the reason behind their fight, but they were both still mad. Ben refused to talk to Logan, and Logan vowed to exclude Ben from his Oscar party guest list when he got famous.

Savannah got down on her knees and began to toss plastic plates and cups back into an over-turned picnic basket. A moment later, Cleopatra was at her side, helping.

"Thanks, Cleo. You're the best."

An offended whine came from Luthor as he turned over on a pile of rolled-up carpets.

"Don't be so sensitive, Luthor. I told you not to eat those lima beans. It's not our fault you got a stomachache."

The monkey tossed in the final napkin ring, and Savannah closed and latched the basket. She hefted it and jammed it onto a high shelf.

And gawked.

There, lined up neatly in the space that had been concealed by the basket, was an array of ran-dom objects — a silver Olympic coin, a cuff link, a tiny bell from a Christmas wreath, a gold pen cap, a rhinestone earring, a shard of broken crystal, and a gleaming black sequin from an old Halloween costume. It was the strangest collection of unre-lated items she'd ever seen. Why, the only thing this stuff had in common was —

When full understanding came to her, Savannah the animal expert sat down in the middle of the floor, gaping in astonishment.

*　　*　　*

Mrs. Bing answered the frantic knocking at the door.

"Savannah, I'm happy to see you, dear, but maybe you shouldn't be here. I know your mother said —"

"I have to talk to Griffin *right now!*" Savannah blurted.

Mrs. Bing was worried. "This is just a friendly call, right? There's been enough trouble already."

"I promise," Savannah swore. "I wouldn't do anything to hurt Griffin."

Mrs. Bing stood aside and Savannah pounded up the stairs. When Griffin heard this, he'd freak. This was the proof that he was innocent!

She knocked. "Griffin! It's me, Savannah!" She threw open the door to reveal The Man With The Plan, sitting on the edge of his bed, staring listlessly at the wall. He looked like he'd been in the same position for the past ten hours.

She dropped the bomb. "Griffin, I know where the ring is!"

Four thousand volts of electricity could not have brought Griffin to his feet faster than this statement. *"Where?"*

"Well, I don't know exactly, but I know what happened to it. Remember that rat in our house? Turns out it was a *pack rat*! A pack rat, Griffin! Isn't that amazing?"

Griffin's face dropped the distance between *I know where the ring is* and *it was a pack rat.* "I'm not following you."

"Listen — pack rats are attracted to shiny objects — like a retainer, or a Super Bowl ring!"

Griffin frowned. "How could a pack rat in your house steal a ring that's at school?"

"I'm not telling it right!" Savannah grabbed two handfuls of her own hair. "Okay — pack rats don't just collect shiny things; they swap their old stuff when they take a new object. What if you lost your retainer at my house — we thought so, remember? The pack rat was attracted by the metal and took it up to the attic. When I was cleaning up the command center, I found his stash — a whole lineup of glittery junk."

Griffin looked puzzled. "But my retainer ended up in the display case at school."

"Here's the thing: Somehow, the pack rat must have crawled into my knapsack, or hidden in my science project or something. That's how he got out of our house. So there he was at school, with the retainer. And what does he see? A big, gold, diamond-studded ring!"

Griffin was skeptical but interested. "How did he get inside a locked display case?"

"He's small," she explained, "and his bones are soft. Rodents can squeeze through a half-inch opening. There's at least double that gap in the case where the two pieces of sliding glass lock together. It would be easy for him to drag the retainer in and the ring out." She fixed him with a piercing stare. "Don't you get it? The ring is in his secret stash, somewhere in the school!"

She expected him to be excited — overjoyed — jumping and cheering. Instead, he lay down on his bed, looking even gloomier than before. His pant leg rode up a little, and she could see the electronic device on his ankle, its indicator light a steady green. She gulped and glanced away.

"Well, I guess anything's possible," he said finally.

"Possible?" Savannah was bewildered. "What's the matter with you? It's a slam dunk! You don't even have to find the ring. Just explain what happened."

"Are you kidding me? That would be like saying the dog ate my homework."

"Dogs don't eat homework," she insisted. "But everybody knows that a pack rat —"

Griffin shook his head sadly. "Not everybody. Only you. Your mind is so into animals that this story is the most obvious thing in the world to you. To anyone else, it's going to seem like an excuse to get myself off the hook — and a crazy one at that. I'd practically be saying that the pack rat planned all this to frame me."

"A pack rat is incapable of advance planning and evil intent," she argued. "You'd be saying that he did what pack rats always do — steal one thing and leave another in its place!"

"If I tell a story like that to Judge Koretsky, my next PEMA bracelet will be around my neck."

She was adamant. "It's not a story. It's what happened. I know it as well as I know my own name."

Griffin sighed. "Pitch has a new suspect, too. She thinks it might be Mr. Clancy because he's still mad at the Jets from nineteen sixty-nine —"

"It's not. I already told you —"

"— and I suppose there's always the others — Vader, Tony . . ." He went on as if no one had spoken.

"Grif-fin!"

But as much as she begged, badgered, and threatened him, he would not accept her pack rat explanation as the truth. To him it was one theory of many, and he didn't try to hide the fact that he considered it to be the wildest of the bunch.

By the time Savannah left the Bing house, she was feeling even lower than Griffin, her feet dragging on the pavement. She had seen him discouraged, flustered, disappointed, intimidated, terrified, and even in the depths of despair. But she had never — not once — seen The Man With The Plan give up.

21

The green warning light on the PEMA bracelet began to flash the instant Griffin stepped off the curb. He pulled up the leg of his jeans and watched with a kind of self-torturing fascination. He didn't want to see it, but he couldn't look away, counting one-Mississippi, two-Mississippi. . . . Sure enough, after ten-Mississippi, the blinking green turned to a solid red.

"Cover that up!" hissed Mrs. Bing.

"It's okay if I'm going to school."

"We don't have to advertise this mess to the entire neighborhood," his mother pleaded.

Griffin nodded bitterly. "Right, we've got Celia White for that." Her column in Monday's *Herald* pretty much implied that Cedarville's notorious "tween gangsters" had tried to mug Dr. Evil inside

Konrad's to steal the brooch. The woman had to be the worst reporter in history. Where did she get her facts? Even Egan wouldn't tell a dumb lie like that. "Look, Mom, I'm fine. Well, maybe not fine, but the anklet's red, and the SWAT team hasn't come to arrest me yet. You don't have to hold my hand all the way to the bus."

"I'm sorry, Griffin. I guess I can't help blaming myself for all this."

Griffin was horrified. "You didn't do anything!"

"Maybe that's the problem," she sniffed. "It's a mother's job to see to it that nothing happens to her child. But you're twelve years old. I can't protect you the way I did when you were three."

Griffin never thought he'd yearn to be a little kid again, yet being three sounded pretty sweet to him now. Too young to be sent to Jail For Kids; too young to stand before a judge. Those were definitely the good old days.

At school, he went straight to the office, as per Vizzini's instructions. Even the grandmotherly secretaries looked tougher at JFK, their expressions unforgiving, their lips thin with disapproval.

"My name is Griffin Bing. I'm supposed to ask you to let the police know I arrived."

Even in this terrible place, where just about everyone was under a cloud, he stood out as the worst of the worst. How had his life come to this?

The morning was lonelier than usual. Sheldon Brickhaus had been standoffish lately. Griffin should have been relieved, almost happy, but it wasn't working out that way. Shank was psycho, but he was also company. And Griffin was coming to realize that even creepy, dangerous company was better than none at all — especially in a place where the hours passed like months.

By lunchtime, he was physically and emotionally exhausted just from the effort of keeping himself awake. As he crossed the cafeteria, he noticed that his shoelace was loose and flapping. It might have been like this all morning for all he knew or cared.

He set down his tray, lifted his foot to the bench, and grabbed the laces. It was in the middle of tying the bow that he heard the buzz in the cafeteria.

All eyes were on him — not on his face, but on his ankle. The leg of his pants had crept up, revealing the PEMA bracelet with its solid red warning light.

He ate his lunch in stiff-necked misery. How could he have been stupid enough to show the anklet to the whole school? Especially here, where every last one of them knew exactly what it was and what it meant. How could you hit bottom and then keep going straight down?

As the period drew to a close, several students exiting the lunchroom — the cream of the JFK crop, toughest of the tough — made a point of passing by his table. Nobody said a word, but their respectful nods were unmistakable.

They're acknowledging me — accepting me!

The only thing worse than attending Jail For Kids was belonging there!

At the end of the line was Shank himself. "You're some piece of work, Justice. You're bad, you're good; you're guilty, you're innocent. And now this. What am I supposed to make of that little piece of bling on your leg?"

"What's it to you?" Griffin mumbled, tight-lipped.

The burly boy's eyes narrowed. "You know what I think? You're a spy! JFK planted you here to rat on the inmates they can't control — like me."

Griffin felt a stab of fear. He could only imagine

what would happen to him if a rumor like *that* got around. "I'm no spy!" he insisted.

"Then explain it for the dumb people!" Shank pressed the tread of his construction boot against the PEMA bracelet. "How does a Boy Scout like you earn one of these?"

Griffin had resolved to share absolutely nothing with his fellow students at JFK — as if revealing a single molecule of his life might make the nightmare real. But once he started to tell the truth, it was a tsunami. He spilled his guts — how the lost retainer in the display case had convinced everyone that Griffin had stolen the Super Bowl ring; how Operations Justice and Stakeout — designed to prove his innocence — had only served to make him look even more guilty; and how none of the other suspects — human or rodent — seemed to be panning out.

As Shank listened to this tale of woe, a smirk began to appear on his cinder-block features. And the more miserable, desperate, and tragic the narrator became, the wider the smile grew, until Sheldon Brickhaus was positively beaming.

Griffin was outraged far beyond the point where he could worry what Shank might do to him. "You're sick, you know that? This is the first time I've ever seen you smile, and it's only because somebody else's life is totally ruined! Thanks a lot!"

"I'm not smiling because you're in trouble," the burly boy cackled. "I'm smiling because you're *lucky*!"

"Lucky?" Griffin seethed. "I'm going on trial for something I didn't even do! And I'll be found guilty for sure, because nobody's ever going to believe what happened. The only thing that could get me off the hook is the ring!"

Shank took Griffin by the shoulders, shaking him like a rag doll. "You're so stupid, Justice — I love that about you! You can't see the forest for the trees! *Think!* A pack rat — don't you know what that is? It's *nuisance wildlife*!"

Griffin stared at him. "You *bought* that fruit-cake idea? You think a pack rat found my retainer, got carried to school with it, and then swapped it for the ring?"

"Nuisance wildlife is my family's bread and butter, man! What you just described — that's practically Pack Rat Behavior One-oh-one."

Griffin was thunderstruck. Of all possible explanations of what had happened to the ring — the original four suspects and the Jets-hating custodian — Savannah's pack rat theory was by far the craziest. Yet here was Shank acting like it was the most obvious thing in the world.

The burly boy was pink with exhilaration. "My old man goes up against pack rats and a whole lot worse every day — and I've been watching him for fourteen years! I could catch a pack rat standing on my head!"

"But —" Griffin had given zero thought to Savannah's rodent story because never in a million years could he have imagined that it might be true. Now his brain was rebooting, examining the problem from every possible angle. "But even if you catch the pack rat, you won't have the ring. That could be anywhere."

Shank dismissed this with a wave of his ham-sized hand. "Once I've got him, I can make him lead me to the ring. This is *doable*, Justice."

Griffin regarded his tormentor in suspicion. There was no trace of malice or trickery in Shank's face. For whatever reason, this bully honestly wanted to help him. Still, he had to ask. "What's in this for you? What do you care about clearing my name?"

Shank nodded slowly, as if he himself wasn't sure of the answer. "We Brickhauses — we're not exactly a high-achieving family. We don't *excel*, as the teachers say. In fact, we stink at pretty much everything. But *this* is what we do. For Bill Gates, it's computers. For us, it's nuisance wildlife. What are the odds that the skill set you need is going to turn out to be what I've got? A million to one? That's destiny, Justice. It's meant to be."

For the first time, Griffin noticed something familiar in Shank's cement features. It was something he normally saw only when looking in a mirror — the energized excitement of a scheme coming together.

Griffin and Shank had something in common.

The scourge of Jail For Kids was a *planner*!

B en dragged his feet all the way home from school. Without Griffin walking by his side, the trip was depressing and arduously uphill. Ferret Face may have been the master of the wake-up nip, but he was no replacement for your best friend.

In science, Ben's new lab partner turned out to be Darren Vader. Like life minus Griffin wasn't hard enough, Ben had to be paired with one of the possible reasons Griffin was gone in the first place — if it didn't turn out to be Tony or Celia White or Dr. Evil, or even Mr. Clancy.

Just thinking about the suspect list made his head spin.

"I can't risk getting acid on my hands during football season," Darren had announced today.

So Ben did all the work while his partner studied the Seahawks' playbook. Ben could never bring himself to stand up to Vader, Griffin-style. It was reason number 147 why he needed Griffin back — after *Always admits he's cheating at Monopoly* but before *Juvie is no place for the greatest friend in the history of the world.*

He could see his house, but he wasn't anxious to get there, even after a long day at school. Most of the allure of his front door lay in the knowledge that, sooner or later, Griffin would be knocking at it.

Now Ben wasn't sure that would ever happen again.

A boy wearing construction boots sat on the front walk, dismantling an anthill with king-sized heels. Ben was amazed he hadn't noticed the newcomer sooner. He was not much taller than Ben himself, but the kid was built like an M1 tank — massive and muscular, with a large, square, crew-cut head.

Spying Ben, he stood. His brawny frame was as wide as it was tall. "You're Slovak, right? I recognize the weasel in your shirt."

"Ferret," Ben corrected nervously, all while

thinking, *Who is this hulk, and what does he want with me?*

The newcomer grabbed his hand and squeezed. "Sheldon Brickhaus. We've got a mutual friend."

Light dawned on Ben. This was Shank from JFK! Crushed fingers were a small price to pay in exchange for a lifeline to Griffin.

"Is Griffin okay?" Ben asked.

Shank let go and stomped on some escaping ants. "He told me to bring you up to speed on the plan."

The plan! Never before had those words been such music to Ben's ears. Had Griffin actually found a way out of this black hole?

"There's a plan?" he barely whispered.

The reply was a slap on the back that very nearly knocked him flat.

"Welcome to Operation Dirty Rat."

BRAINSTORMING MEETING – DUKAKIS HOUSE – 8:45 p.m.

In attendance: SLOVAK, Ben; BENSON, Pitch; KELLERMAN, Logan; DRYSDALE, Savannah; DUKAKIS, Melissa; BRICKHAUS, Sheldon; FACE, Ferret; LUTHOR.

Via videoconference: BING, Griffin

Shank was completely unruffled when Luthor approached him with teeth bared. "Cute puppy," he commented mildly.

"Why did you bring the dog?" Ben asked Savannah. The Doberman was a fact of life at the Drysdales', but he expected Melissa's house to be Luthor-free.

"It was the only way I could get out," Savannah explained. "My parents are all over me except when I'm taking care of the animals."

The team sat in a circle on the floor of the small bedroom. Melissa, the hostess, started the meeting with the click of a mouse. Griffin's face appeared on her laptop screen.

"Thanks for coming, everybody," he greeted them. "Guys, meet Shank. Shank — the team. Now, we all know there's a possibility that Savannah's pack rat is at school, and that he's got the Super Bowl ring hidden there somewhere. The objective of Operation Dirty Rat is to catch him and get him to lead us to his stash."

"And we do this *how*?" asked Pitch in amazement.

"Piece of cake," Shank said confidently. "It's kind of a family tradition for us Brickhauses." He helped himself to a potato chip from a big bowl and tossed one to Luthor, who caught it in midair.

"Shank's our nuisance wildlife specialist," Griffin informed them. "He'll be running the operation with me."

"With *you*?" echoed Savannah. "You're under house arrest. How are you free to go rat catching at the middle school?"

Melissa supplied the answer. "Griffin's PEMA hub transmits a unique code to a monitoring system in the police station. If I can hack in and clone that code, I might be able to rig a pocket transmitter to send the same signal."

"Which will tell the police I'm at home being a good little boy," Griffin finished.

Melissa nodded. "So long as the unit is within range of the bracelet. Which it will be, since you'll keep it with you."

"What about the rest of us?" asked Savannah.

"The school's never empty," Griffin told them. "Teachers and administrators come in at odd hours to work on things. They can't find out we're there ring hunting. And don't forget Mr. Clancy. Remember — there might be more than one rat in this scenario. Just because we're after the rodent doesn't mean we've eliminated the other suspects. We have to be careful."

"What do you want us to do?" asked Pitch. "Create a diversion?"

Shank shook his head seriously. "We need more time than that. First we have to catch the pack rat. Then we have to follow him to the ring."

"No diversion lasts that long," Ben agreed darkly.

"Except one," Logan put in. *"Hail Caesar."*

Griffin frowned. "The school play?"

"Wednesday is opening night," Logan enthused.

"But the school will be full of people!" Ben protested.

"People watching the play," Logan amended.

"Not when they're going to the bathroom."

Logan assumed an expression of haughty dignity. "I have created a Julius Caesar so riveting, so multidimensional that no one will be going to the bathroom. For my Caesar, they'll hold it in."

Shank regarded Logan oddly. "Is this kid for real?"

Pitch nodded. "He does a scooter wipeout that could win a Golden Globe."

"It's perfect," Griffin decided. "Logan's play is

our cover. Melissa's on electronics, Shank handles nuisance wildlife, and we've got Savannah as our rodent behavior expert. Pitch on climbing; Ben for tight spaces. It's a plan!"

They went around the circle. All groundings and punishments would be over by Wednesday, all team members ready and willing. There were nods of agreement and determined grunts of "We're in" and "Let's do it."

Shank was impressed. "Man, I thought I was in the middle of a dweeb convention! You guys are my kind of people!"

An uneasy murmur was punctuated by the smack of Luthor's tongue as he helped himself to the rest of the chips.

None of them wanted to be Shank's kind of people.

OPERATION DIRTY RAT - EQUIPMENT LIST

9 (nine) animal traps - Shank

1 (one) rodent harness - Savannah

1 (one) climbing rope - Pitch

3 (three) walkie-talkies - Griffin

1 (one) fishing rod . . .

G riffin put down the notebook, trying to blink away a pounding headache. Operation Dirty Rat had not yet even begun, and he was already stressed. There were so many fine points that needed to be ironed out before zero hour on Wednesday. His parents, for example. They'd never let him leave while under house arrest, and sneaking out was no good, either — not for hours. What if they checked his room and found it empty?

No, Mom and Dad had to be sent away some-place. But where, and for what reason?

A single blown detail could bring the entire operation crashing down around his ears. Hard experience had taught Griffin this.

The planning session was taking place at the ping-pong table in the basement, while Melissa probed with a screwdriver inside the PEMA hub, which was bolted to the floor. That was another source of his jitters. One false move could alert the police.

Chill out, he soothed himself. *Melissa knows what she's doing. . . .*

Her voice was so soft that he almost missed it. "Ready," she announced.

"Really? That's — uh — great. Are you sure? I mean — uh — *what's* ready?"

She held out an old cell phone with the backing removed and the wiring exposed. "This handset generates a digital signal that matches the hub on the floor. If you shut down the hub and turn this on, it will transmit to the police station directly. We have to test it, of course."

"Of course." Griffin accepted the device, han-dling it as if it were filled with nitroglycerin. He had faith in Melissa, but he didn't relish the prospect of more face time with Detective Sergeant Vizzini.

She read his mind. "Well, if it doesn't work, better to know now than on Wednesday night," she reasoned. "If the police get an alarm signal, you'll be home. They'll figure it's a glitch in their system."

Griffin took a deep breath. "Okay, on three. One . . . two . . ." He powered on the converted cell phone at the same instant that Melissa clicked off the hub.

The transmit light on the floor unit winked out. Griffin's heart jumped up the back of his throat. But —

He pulled up his pant leg and checked the indicator on the PEMA anklet. Solid green.

They waited. Three minutes. Then five. No sirens in the distance. No insistent pounding at the front door.

"It works?" he asked.

"I think so," she told him. "In here. Now we have to try it outside the hub's range."

Right. Who cared if the device did the trick in the house, where Griffin was allowed to be anyway? The real test would be to take it beyond the two-hundred-foot limit.

They headed upstairs. Mom was out and Dad was in his workshop, experimenting with different bait trays for the Vole-B-Gone. They were safe for the moment — so long as a stray police car didn't pass by.

"Let's go."

Griffin wasn't sure why he was so afraid to walk on his own lawn. He did this every morning en route to the JFK bus. The anklet wouldn't begin to flash its warning until he reached the road.

He clung to the transmitter with white knuckles. If Melissa was right, the device would trick the PEMA system into thinking he was still in the house.

He stepped down to the blacktop. Anklet check: no blinking.

Two more strides took him to the middle of the street. Nothing. He crossed the road and jogged onto the opposite lawn. The anklet was now at least a hundred feet out of range, and the indicator still showed solid green.

It works! It really works!

Since the cell phone was now acting as the hub, all he had to do was hold on to it. He could be miles from home, yet the device would never be far from the bracelet on his ankle — well inside the two-hundred-foot limit.

"Melissa," he called, his voice low despite the triumph he felt. "You're a genius."

Her eyes were covered by her curtain of hair, but her lips betrayed a rare smile.

A loud mechanical clanking disturbed the quiet of the block. Griffin watched in horror as the Bings' garage door began to open. He saw his father's shoes . . . pants . . . shirt — in another second, the whole guy would be standing there with a perfect view of his house-arrested son!

Griffin dashed across the street and up the walk in a desperate bid to outrun the rising door. He flung himself inside just as the mechanism clicked off, and Mr. Bing stepped onto the driveway.

"Oh, hi, Melissa," he said, noticing the shy girl. "I didn't know you were coming over."

"I was just leaving," she told him before starting for home.

Her work there was done.

24

At two o'clock on Wednesday afternoon — zero hour minus five — Mr. Bing was at his computer, browsing through farm blogs. For people who worked from dawn till dusk, farmers certainly seemed to be quite an online community, always willing to share their expertise. But no one seemed to have any idea what bait to use to trap the orchard vole.

His frustration had been growing in recent weeks. The SmartPick and Rollo-Bushel were both fully operational. If he could only perfect the Vole-B-Gone, it would round out his resume as an inventor and establish him as a major player in the orchard world.

He chuckled ruefully. The voles, apparently, had other plans.

A chime alerted him to the arrival of a new

e-mail. He called up his inbox. The message was from Dalton Davis of Davis, Davis, and Yamamoto, the law firm the family had hired to represent Griffin.

Mr. and Mrs. Bing:

I would like to confer with you as soon as possible on the subject of a break in your son's case. As I'm in court all afternoon, would it be possible to meet at the Four Corners diner at 7:30 p.m? I apologize for the short notice, but I think you'll be pleased with the outcome.

Dalton Davis

"Honey!" he called excitedly to his wife. "Come and see this!"

Mrs. Bing hurried into the room. "A break in the case!" she repeated. "That sounds hopeful!"

The Bings had no illusions about their son. Griffin was capable of spectacular mischief and had proven it more than once. But to see him go down for something he hadn't even done was the ultimate torture. Could this be the first ray of hope to penetrate the black cloud that had surrounded the family for weeks now?

Eagerly, Mr. Bing typed a short reply: *Thanks — we'll be there.* They had met at this roadside restaurant before. It was located about halfway between Cedarville and the offices of Davis, Davis, and Yamamoto in New York City.

The couple joined hands. The shadow over their son's future was almost unbearable. But perhaps there was light at the end of the tunnel.

Mrs. Bing's eyes fell on the folded copy of the *Herald* on the desk beside the mouse pad. Celia White's column was on the front page. The headline read:

CMS VISITS ANCIENT ROME WITH *HAIL CAESAR*

Her melancholy returned. "The school play," she said sadly. "While we're meeting with lawyers, fighting for Griffin's life, other parents will be bundling their kids into costumes and watching them perform."

Her husband nodded unhappily. "The worst part is seeing him locked in the house like a criminal. That used to be his school. Now he can't even buy a ticket and go to their play."

What Mr. and Mrs. Bing did not know was that Griffin was very much going to the school that night — not to watch the play, but to lead the team in Operation Dirty Rat. And the e-mail they believed was from their lawyer had actually come from the laptop of Melissa Dukakis.

TONIGHT — 7 P.M.
CEDARVILLE MIDDLE SCHOOL
PROUDLY PRESENTS

HAIL CAESAR
A TRAGIC STORY OF POWER AND BETRAYAL

STARRING

JULIUS CAESAR.................LOGAN KELLERMAN

MARK ANTONY . . .

Okay, there were other names on the welcome poster that hung in the entrance foyer. Mrs. Arturo insisted that the entire cast had to be on there — right down to the lowliest centurion and set painter.

But Logan only had eyes for himself. Julius Caesar. After mindless kiddie shows and dumb commercials for athlete's foot cream, here at last was a role meaty enough for him to sink his teeth into. Today was the first day of the rest of his life as an actor. He had to *nail* this performance. Absolutely nothing could be allowed to interfere with his dramatic focus.

Out of the corner of his eye, he noticed a tiny shadow with a long skinny tail moving quickly across the terrazzo floor, hugging the wall.

A rat! A *pack* rat? Could Savannah's wacky theory be true?

He launched himself across the foyer on an intercept course with the fleeing creature.

At that moment, the heavy glass doors opened, and a tall woman rushed into the building. Logan collided with the newcomer and bounced off, dazed.

"What on earth?" she exclaimed in outrage.

"Sorry —" He took in her familiar birdlike features.

Oh, no! Celia White!

"You're Logan, right?" The reporter skewered him with hawk eyes. "What happened to your face? You look like you've been in a knife fight!"

"It's — uh — makeup," he stammered. "Caesar was a general before he was an emperor, you know."

Her expression softened. "I'm proud of you,

Logan. I know you've been in trouble in the past. To see you starring in the play is wonderful!"

Logan could only stare at her.

"I was right all along," the reporter went on. "Once that awful Griffin Bing was removed from the mix, the rest of you could start to turn your lives around. Sometimes you have to cut off one bad branch to save the whole tree. I only hope your other friends can find such positive outlets for their energy." She reached out a claw and shook his hand. "Congratulations. I'll be in the front row cheering for you." And she stalked off to reserve a good seat.

Logan was still shaking as she disappeared down the corridor that led to the auditorium. The only "positive outlet" his friends had found was Operation Dirty Rat, which would be starting any minute. And this time, the team was bringing along the worst juvenile delinquent at Jail For Kids. What would Celia White have to say about that?

A quick scan of the foyer revealed no sign of the rodent. Just as well. He mustn't allow himself to get distracted. Not on opening night.

Hail *Caesar* was a sellout. By 6:45, the parking lot of Cedarville Middle School was jam-packed, and both sides of the street were lined with cars to accommodate the spillover.

The school's front foyer was a mob scene as student ushers rushed to show the throngs of theatergoers to the auditorium in time for the play to begin on schedule.

One small group, however, kept its distance from the bustling school building. In the darkness of the deserted football field, Savannah, Pitch, Melissa, Ben, and Shank milled around one of the goalposts, waiting for The Man With The Plan to arrive.

Ben was fiddling nervously with the reel of his father's fishing rod. "It's not like him to be late. What if the transmitter-thingy messed up? He could be in jail right now."

"He's not," Melissa said quietly. "It worked perfectly when we tested it."

Shank hefted the canvas bag containing nine of his father's rodent traps. "He gets five more minutes. Then we start without him."

Nobody uttered a sound. The only thing worse than being on a plan without Griffin was being anywhere with Sheldon Brickhaus.

In the next moment, Griffin was among them, breathless from running. "Sorry, guys," he panted. "I had to wait for my folks to leave for the fake meeting."

He felt guilty about how upbeat Mom and Dad had been. They were so hopeful that his troubles might soon be over. They were going to be devastated when Dalton Davis was a no-show at the diner. His one consolation was the fact that he hadn't been lying when the e-mail had promised "a break in the case." If Operation Dirty Rat went well, there'd be no case left to break.

Pitch pointed to the modified cell phone firmly attached to Griffin's belt. "Is that *it*?" she asked, adjusting the coil of climbing rope she carried over her shoulder.

Griffin nodded. "And it stays with me no matter what. It's the same deal as the hub in my basement.

If it falls off and I get out of its range, you'll be visiting me in the slammer."

The sound of distant applause reached them, along with the majestic opening music of *Hail Caesar*. That meant everyone was in the auditorium. The coast was clear.

The play was on, and so was Operation Dirty Rat.

The team entered the building cautiously. The foyer and halls were deserted, but no one could rule out the chance of a stray wanderer — including Mr. Clancy, Dr. Egan, or Celia White, who was covering the play for the *Herald*. Both Darren Vader and Tony Bartholomew had been spotted in the ticket line. All the suspects were on the scene. Including, Griffin hoped, one very guilty pack rat.

Shank led the group down the corridor, stopping at a small alcove between the two bathrooms. From his bag, he produced a cage trap the size of half a shoe box and placed it against the wall in the corner, underneath a porcelain drinking fountain. The bars were bent and stained with age, and holes in the mesh had been repaired with staples and window screening. It was a piece of junk compared with the brand-new, high-tech Vole-B-Gone, but Griffin didn't dare use his father's invention. If pack rats found the prototype as easy to avoid as voles did, he'd be out of luck.

Shank reached into his pocket, pulled out a crystal spray bottle of perfume, and squeezed four big blasts into the small enclosure.

Instantly, a powerful, sickly sweet floral odor was all around them.

Ben nearly dropped the rod. "What's that — Eau de Dead Body?"

Shank grinned. "It's called Rendezvous in Paris."

Pitch choked. "I feel like I'm drinking a Shirley Temple inside a sewage treatment plant."

"My mother used it one morning," Shank explained. "And when my dad got to work, the animals were all over him. Turns out no nuisance wildlife can resist it."

As if to prove this point, a tiny nose poked out the bottom of Ben's shirt, sniffing furiously. A second later, Ferret Face burst into the open in a swan dive onto the cage.

Ben scooped up the ferret and stuffed him back under his collar. "Don't even think about it, pal. You're not a nuisance — most of the time."

Savannah removed a glittery ball of aluminum foil from her backpack and placed it inside the trap. "Because pack rats like shiny things," she explained.

Shank nodded approvingly. "Let's set the rest of these traps."

As the team headed off after Shank, Griffin patted the transmitter on his belt and checked the indicator light on his PEMA anklet. Still green.

So far, so good.

The Bings stepped into the Four Corners diner and looked around. The dining room was crowded, but there was no sign of Dalton Davis.

Mr. Bing sensed his wife's unease. "He's probably just stuck in traffic. It's murder getting out of the city this time of day." He turned to the hostess. "Table for three, please. We're meeting someone."

They sat down, and the waitress brought them two coffees.

"Just what I need," commented Mrs. Bing with a nervous smile. "Something to make me even more jittery."

Their eyes never wavered from the front door.

Both cups remained untouched.

*　　*　　*

The lofty pillars of ancient Rome towered over Logan Kellerman. Well, they weren't *real* pillars — just background scenery painted on huge art paper and held up by tall wooden frames.

But for a true actor, that was all it took. He was no longer a seventh grader; he was Gaius Julius Caesar, Rome's greatest general, speaking before the Senate. Dressed in a toga and sandals, he projected to the last seat in the last row of the auditorium.

"The victory of our legions in Gaul has brought greater glory and riches to the Republic . . . !"

As he delivered the speech, his eyes panned the crowd, settling briefly on Darren Vader in the second row. For some reason, Darren was holding up a file card. Logan squinted to make out the message: NICE DRESS.

The insult almost caused Logan to garble the word *maximus*. But he recovered and concentrated on his proud parents in the front row beside Celia White. The newspaper columnist was beaming up at him. She may have been a dangerous lunatic, but at least she appreciated good theater.

A few rows behind her fidgeted Tony, looking nervous and squirming in his chair. Was that because he was up to something?

His eyes traveled to Dr. Egan, who was not in a seat, but standing at the back of the auditorium. Every now and then, he would open the door a crack and peer out into the hall. Looking for latecomers, Logan reasoned. But he hoped Griffin and the team would be careful.

The team placed all nine traps — three on the second floor, three on the main floor, and three in the basement. Then came the hard part — watching and waiting. They broke into pairs. Savannah and Melissa took the upstairs post; Griffin and Shank stayed on the ground level; and Pitch and Ben were sent down the custodians' steps to the boiler room.

"How come we get stuck with dungeon duty?" Ben whined over the walkie-talkie. "It's creepy. There could be rats down here."

"That's what we're hoping for," Griffin told him nervously. "One, anyway — the one with the ring."

"All clear up top," Pitch reported. "I mean, it smells like a funeral parlor, but the traps are still empty."

"You know," Melissa's quiet voice came over the small speaker, "when our house had squirrel problems, it took a few days before the snares caught anything."

"That's because her nuisance wildlife guy didn't know about Rendezvous in Paris," Shank assured Griffin. "The stuff is the gold standard. Trust me. It won't be long."

The time passed nerve-rackingly slowly. Griffin could hear a lot of action coming from the auditorium — a battle scene, maybe. He pictured Logan, in Julius Caesar's plastic armor, fighting with a toy sword.

Shank found his own way to keep himself entertained. He snatched the transmitter from Griffin's belt, cocked back his arm, and asked, "Hey, do you think I can chuck this more than two hundred feet?"

Griffin was in full panic. "Are you crazy? If that thing breaks, I'm dead!"

Shank was disgusted. "I don't know why I hang out with you, Justice," he said, returning the unit. "Where's your sense of humor? You're as much fun as the chicken pox."

Griffin was about to retort when another sound reached them, different from the play, and closer. Footsteps.

"Radio silence!" he whispered frantically into the walkie-talkie. "Someone's coming!"

Shank grabbed Griffin and hauled him around the corner into the boys' room. There they hid, barely daring to breathe, as the rhythmic tapping of leather on terrazzo grew louder and louder. Then they saw him, heading down the main hall to the office.

Mr. Clancy.

His usual work shirt had been replaced by a Colts jersey, matching the colors of his head-band. Griffin was turned to stone. Was the custodian all decked out in his team regalia to take his final revenge on the '69 Jets? To make some kind of move on the ring, or even get rid of it altogether?

And here we are in the middle of a risky plan to trap the wrong suspect!

The custodian passed by, heading toward the office.

"It's Clancy," Griffin breathed into the walkie-talkie.

"I knew it!" hissed Pitch. "Has he got the ring?"

"Not yet," Griffin whispered.

"What should we *do*?" quavered Melissa's voice.

Griffin's eyes met Shank's in wordless question.

"Sit tight and be ready to move," the older boy advised. "If we spot the ring on him, we can't let the guy out of the building."

It was only a few minutes, but it seemed like hours, before the footsteps returned.

Trembling, Griffin peered out the doorway of the bathroom.

Something small was cradled in the custodian's hands. Florescent lighting glinted off a shiny surface.

The words were almost out of Griffin's mouth: *Red alert* —

Then he recognized the object — a foil-wrapped candy bar.

He tried to wheeze "False alarm!" into the walkie-talkie, but no sound came out. The enormity of the mistake he'd nearly made threatened to tear him in two. If he hadn't been leaning against the boys' room wall, he probably would have collapsed under legs of jelly.

Mr. Clancy walked by once again in the direction of the auditorium. Soon the footsteps faded.

"All clear," Griffin murmured into the walkie-talkie. He stepped toward the door.

Shank put an iron grip on his shoulder. "Don't move."

Heart thumping, Griffin followed Shank's pointing finger. In the hall outside the bathroom, a small shape was slinking along the baseboard in the direction of the drinking fountain. The light brown creature was small, furry, and round as a baseball.

Behind the body trailed a long rodent tail.

The pack rat.

Savannah was right!

Of course she was right. This was the girl who had taken the meanest guard dog on Long Island and turned him into her best friend. When it came to animals, Savannah Drysdale was money in the bank.

Griffin and Shank watched, mesmerized, as the little rodent sniffed his way up to the trap. An inch before the opening, he hesitated, weighing the pros and cons — the irresistible scent of Rendezvous in Paris versus the danger of the unknown. The shiny ball of foil seemed to sway the decision. In a single bound, he raced into the cage, snatched up the prize, and turned to make his exit.

Too late. The door snapped shut, cutting off his escape.

"We've got him," Griffin breathed into the walkie-talkie. "He's in the trap."

"Mr. Clancy?" Ben asked in amazement.

"The dirty rat is caught," said The Man With The Plan.

By eight o'clock, there was still no sign of Dalton Davis at the Four Corners diner, and the Bings were nearly frantic.

Mr. Bing was pacing in the parking lot, talking on his cell phone with the switchboard at Davis, Davis, and Yamamoto. When he returned to his wife, his face was gray.

"Dalton Davis is at the opera."

Mrs. Bing was devastated. "The opera? Then why on earth would the man tell us to —" Light dawned. "There was never any meeting, was there?"

Her husband shook his head grimly. "We've been hoodwinked."

"But by *who*?" she demanded.

When the answer came to them, they both blurted it out in near unison. *"Griffin!"*

Mr. Bing tossed some bills on the table and joined his wife in a mad dash for the van.

*   *   *

The pack rat cowered in the trap, hugging the ball of foil to his belly, peering furtively out at the six team members who now surrounded him.

So this was the guilty party, the lowdown punk who had stolen Art Blankenship's Super Bowl ring and framed Griffin in the process. Not Mr. Clancy or Dr. Evil or Celia White or Tony. Not even Vader, Griffin's worst enemy. This tiny, frightened rodent.

Savannah rubbed at moist eyes. "He's just so small and scared and helpless. We must seem like giants to him. Look — he's protecting the ball of foil. We outweigh him by a factor of a thousand, yet he's standing up for what's his. How honorable is that?"

"You can't have honor if you go to the bathroom in the same place where you sleep," Pitch put in. "No offense, Ferret Face," she added to the head poking out of Ben's collar.

"Assuming he's the thief, this little monster almost got me thrown in juvie," Griffin reminded them darkly. "It might still happen if we can't pull this off."

"You can't blame an animal for following its natural instinct," Savannah insisted.

195

"You can if it ruins your best friend's life!" Ben snapped back.

"That's why it's called *nuisance* wildlife," Shank explained patiently. "If these critters were a party to hang out with, they'd call it something else."

"We're wasting time," Griffin reminded them. "Let's start Phase Two."

Shank popped the cage door and reached inside, but the frightened pack rat slipped away from his meaty hand. Several more attempts yielded the same result.

Savannah elbowed him out of the way. "He's petrified." From her pocket, she removed a restaurant-sized peanut butter packet, smeared a small streak across her palm, and held it just inside the trap. "All right, cutie-pie. Here's a treat for you."

The anxious rodent hesitated, clinging to the ball of foil as if trying to hide behind it.

"It's okay," she crooned.

When Savannah resorted to this tone, she was like Dr. Dolittle. No animal could resist. Sure enough, the pack rat abandoned his prize and went for the peanut butter, whiskers twitching.

She drew the little creature up and out, petting him gently as he lapped at the snack. Then, with her free hand, she drew a tiny leather harness from her backpack and slipped it over the head and front paws.

"I'm not even going to ask why you own a thing like that," Pitch commented.

"I sized it down from a Chihuahua leash so I could exercise my hamsters," Savannah explained.

"Couldn't you just put them on one of those wheels?" Ben asked curiously.

"Running on a wheel is pointless," Savannah replied with contempt, "and they know it. It depresses them."

Shank took the fishing rod from Ben, tied the end of the line onto the harness, and began to unspool the reel.

Savannah set the pack rat down. "Okay, cutie-pie. Lead us home."

Toenails scrambling on the hard floor, the creature took off down the hall, with the team in pursuit. Shank was in the lead, reeling like mad, increasing the speedy rodent's head start, but keeping it in visual range.

Griffin was right on his heels, breathing a silent prayer with every step. If Mr. Clancy went for another snack break, there'd be no avoiding him this time.

"How do we know he's going to take us to the ring?" puffed Melissa, struggling to keep pace.

"An animal in danger heads toward safety," Savannah panted in reply. "For a pack rat, that's his stash."

Bounced and jostled by the furious activity, Ferret Face became agitated, emitting a series of wild clucks.

Ben recognized the warning signs all too well. "Oh, no you don't! No throwing up tonight!" He set the ferret down beside him, and the two of them rejoined the chase.

By now, the pack rat had opened up a sixty-foot lead. He turned left, feet skittering, and disappeared around the corner. Instinctively, Shank yanked back on the line, bringing their quarry to a jarring halt.

Horrified, Savannah smacked his hand. "How'd you like to be manhandled by a force a hundred times your own strength?"

Shank stared at her. He was not used to being slapped. But he obediently paid out more slack, and the pack rat was off again. The team wheeled around the bend after him.

A right turn sent them racing through the heart

of the school, past the gym, toward the auditorium. They could hear music from the play and snippets of dialogue. Griffin thought he recognized Logan's strident voice, but this was no time to lose concentration. The plan had entered its most critical phase and also the most delicate. On the other side of the wall sat hundreds of people. It would only take one audience member en route to the bathroom to sink Operation Dirty Rat.

The pack rat bolted down a side hall, scurrying past a chair that was propping open a heavy metal door. Shank hurdled the obstacle, but the fishing line wrapped under the seat, sending it tumbling into the back of his legs. He tripped and went down, losing his grip on the rod. With a buzzing noise, the reel paid out as the fugitive rodent darted away. Shank clamped his hand on the spool and locked it. Scrambling up again, he rejoined the chase. The door, now free, shut behind him.

Pitch was running so hard that her momentum carried her right into it. She bounced off, wrenching at the handle. The door wouldn't budge.

Griffin sprinted onto the scene. "Let's move!" he rasped.

"It's locked!" she hissed back.

"You mean we've *lost* them?" gasped Ben, scooping up Ferret Face, who was scratching at the metal.

"I don't trust anybody who thinks wildlife is a nuisance," Savannah added urgently. "It's *people* who are a nuisance to animals!"

"Never mind that!" Griffin hissed. He was in a full panic, jerking the handle as if he believed he could tear the steel dead bolt clear of its housing. "That pack rat is our only connection to the ring! We've got to find him!"

"How are we going to do that?" Ben demanded. "Shank's got no walkie-talkie, and we can't exactly yell the school down!"

"There must be some way to figure out where they went." Pitch looked around desperately. "Where does this door lead, anyway?"

Julius Caesar was in his glory. He had just been named the undisputed leader of the Roman Republic. It was his greatest triumph. And Logan was experiencing a triumph of his own — to ace a role before a spellbound crowd hundreds strong.

"Citizens of Rome, I stand before you in all humility. . . ."

Man, this was going well! The people in the front row were practically on their feet, gasping from the effect of his performance. What Logan didn't know was that directly behind him, the pack rat was scampering from wing to wing in full view of the audience.

"Behold the indestructible city we have built together!"

No sooner were the words past his lips than the giant set poster depicting the Circus Maximus exploded and Sheldon Brickhaus blasted onto the stage, fishing rod in hand, thundering after the rat. He knocked over an aqueduct and flattened the Pantheon before crashing through the background scenery of the Seven Hills of Rome. He was gone so quickly it was almost as if he had never even been there — except for the wreckage he'd left in his wake.

Julius Caesar, Rome's greatest general, stood in the ruins of his eternal city. Surely Johnny Depp himself had never faced an acting challenge as enormous as the one Logan found himself confronted with. His next line was supposed to be *"Our beloved Rome will stand for ten thousand years!"* But he couldn't very well say that, could he? *This* Rome hadn't even lasted until the third act.

What words could possibly rescue the play from this terrible disaster?

Julius Caesar turned back to the audience and gave it his best shot: "You know, you just can't get good marble these days!"

The show must go on.

*　　*　　*

Griffin saw the pack rat first and managed to catch up to Shank by the time the burly boy emerged from the backstage corridor. The others converged from all directions, footfalls echoing up and down the halls.

"Where were you?" Griffin panted.

"It's not good," Shank admitted, his usual calm a little ruffled. "Julius Caesar says yo."

"You were in the auditorium?" Ben wheezed. "Did Dr. Evil see you?"

"Everybody saw me! I was on the stage!"

"Oh, no!" moaned Pitch. "Griffin, you better take off. We're about to get caught, and you can't be a part of it!"

"This isn't over yet," Griffin said through clenched teeth. "If we find the ring, getting caught won't matter."

Even the unshakable Shank was starting to get nervous. "She's right, Justice. You're in too deep. Let us take the heat."

Griffin shook his head stubbornly. "If we go down, we go down as a team."

Melissa pointed. "Speaking of going down —"

They stared. The pack rat was making a bee-line for the storage area and the staircase that led to the basement.

The team pounded down the steps after him, Shank in the lead, reeling like mad.

"Don't hurt him!" Savannah begged.

"If I can't keep him close, he's going to lose us in all this junk!" Shank retorted.

They looked around, catching their breath. The basement was filled with broken desks, extra chairs, rolled-up mats, gym equipment, and hundreds of crates and cartons. At the center stood the furnace. An enormous central boiler fed dozens of pipes and ducts leading upward and outward like the gnarled branches of an ancient tree.

The pack rat led them through an obstacle course, jumping expertly from box to stack to crate.

"He knows exactly where he's going!" Savannah marveled in a whisper. "Look how sure he is. He's close to home!"

They watched, transfixed, as their quarry hopped from a file cabinet to the side of the furnace itself. He climbed high on the boiler before detouring onto a pipe, following its length until it disappeared into the suspended ceiling. The last thing they saw was his long, skinny tail being drawn inside.

"That's it," said Shank positively. "His stuff is there."

Savannah nodded. "Definitely."

The nuisance wildlife expert and animal behavior specialist were in agreement.

"Wouldn't you know it," groaned Ben. "How are we supposed to get way up there?"

"That's my department." Pitch adjusted her coil of rope. "One Super Bowl ring coming up." She scrambled along a series of metal rungs on the side of the boiler and then expertly shinnied out onto the pipe, following the path that their quarry had taken. She moved with athletic grace and ease, completely unfazed by the fact that she was suspended more than twenty feet above the basement floor.

Ben craned his neck to track her progress as she worked her way higher on the pipe. "I know she tries stuff twenty times harder when she goes climbing with her family, but this freaks me out. I mean, one wrong move and she's a grease spot on the cement."

"She knows what she's doing," said Griffin, but even he seemed tense watching her operate so high up.

As the pipe steepened to vertical, Pitch met the fishing line that was still attached to the pack rat's harness. She touched it. "He's stopped," she called down. "He must be just inside the ceiling."

Moving slowly now, she inched upward until her hair brushed the suspended ceiling. Then, locking her powerful legs onto the pipe, she carefully moved the tile aside and stuck her head inside for a look.

The crawl space was tight, designed to accommodate ducts, pipes, wires, but certainly not people. A few feet away sat the pack rat, gnawing at the leather strap of the unfamiliar harness. He was surrounded by a vast array of shiny objects — prisms, paper clips, costume jewelry, dozens of colored beads.

And there in the center, pride of the collection, sat Art Blankenship's diamond-studded 1969 New York Jets Super Bowl championship ring.

28

"**J**ackpot!"

Pitch thrust her hand inside the ceiling to pick up the ring, praying that the pack rat was a collector, not a fighter.

Frightened, the little animal backed away until it had reached the end of the slack on the fishing line. There he cowered, wide eyed and quivering, as this huge invader approached his precious stash.

The hand drew closer and closer until it was eight inches from the ring.

"Have you got it?" Griffin asked anxiously.

"I can't reach it," said Pitch in a strained voice.

"Try harder," Griffin begged.

"It's no use. My shoulders are too wide to fit past the ceiling grid. I just need a few more inches. . . ."

"We'll have to send Ben," Griffin decided.

"What — up there?" Ben blurted.

"Pitch doesn't fit, but you will," Griffin explained. "You're our tight spaces specialist."

"Yeah, here on earth. How am I supposed to get up there? Fly?"

It almost came to that. Pitch took the coil of rope from her shoulder and slung it around a horizontal section of heavy pipe, dangling both ends down to the floor. Following her directions, Griffin wrapped one end around Ben's waist and between his legs, forming a strong harness. Like he was going to the gallows, Ben handed Ferret Face over to the only person he trusted to deal with an apprehensive ferret — Savannah. Then Shank and Griffin began to haul on the free end of the rope, winching Ben up toward the ceiling. He had only one request as he was ratcheted higher and higher.

"Don't let go."

Working the makeshift pulley system, Shank regarded him skeptically. "I think your friend up there might be crying."

"Make no mistake," Griffin replied confidently. "Ben complains a lot, but when push comes to shove, he gets the job done. If he stays awake."

"Huh?"

"It's a long story. Keep pulling. Nothing can stop us now."

At that moment, there were pounding footsteps on the stairs, and Darren Vader barreled into the furnace room. "You're busted, suckers! The minute the play got trashed, I knew it had something to do with you!" His eyes bulged as he caught sight of Pitch, perched at the ceiling, and the rising Ben just a few feet below her position. "Okay, I don't get it."

"Beat it, Vader!" Griffin snarled in a strained voice. "This is none of your business!"

"It's the ring, isn't it?" Darren was triumphant. "Great hiding place, Bing! A little extreme maybe, but I give you props for picking a spot nobody's going to look."

Savannah glared daggers at Darren. "Even you can't be mean enough to turn us in, knowing what it'll mean for Griffin."

"I'm not turning anybody in," Darren assured them. "So long as I get my fair share."

"Your fair share of *what*?" Griffin demanded.

"Of the money from when you sell it! I want my cut — plus maybe a little bonus for keeping my mouth shut."

"Nobody's selling anything," came a firm voice behind Darren.

Everyone wheeled. Even Ben managed to dangle in that direction. There stood Tony Bartholomew, a look of grim determination on his face.

"That ring is mine. It's going home with me."

"Mrs. Blankenship donated it to the *school*," Savannah argued. "It was a gift."

"So how come you hid it in the basement ceiling?" Darren challenged.

"Ignore them," Pitch told Ben. "Let's just do our job." She reached down and guided the hanging boy onto the pipe. The young climber didn't think she'd ever seen anyone quite so terrified. "It's no big deal," she soothed him. "It's just high."

Ben was nearly hysterical. "I don't care about the *high*! I'm worried about how fast I could be *low* again!"

She shuffled over and pushed him into the crawl space. "You see the ring, right? If you can just get your shoulders past that wood frame . . ."

Other people had best friends, Ben reflected bitterly. Normal ones, the kind that didn't send a guy into the ceiling of his school's furnace room to burglarize a pack rat. But there was no way around it. Griffin needed this to happen, and Ben was the only one who could get in there. Griffin would do the same for him.

Holding his arms in front of him like a high diver, he made himself small and eased through the opening, the wood frame scraping the skin of his shoulders. He reached for the ring at the center of the collection of trinkets, keeping an eye on the pack rat, who was watching him resentfully.

Just as his fingers closed on Art Blankenship's treasure, the creature darted forward and snatched it with his teeth.

"Hey!"

The pack rat tried to flee, but the fishing line was taut and held him in place a few feet away.

"What's going on?" called Griffin from below.

"I had it," Ben tried to explain, "but the rat took it back!"

"Grab it!" ordered Shank.

"I can't reach him!"

"Not the rat, the fishing line!" Shank yelled. "When we bring you down, he'll have to come with you!"

Ben snatched at the black nylon fiber, wrapping it around his fist so he wouldn't drop it. Then he eased himself out of the crawl space and rasped, "Lower away!"

Griffin and Shank began to ease on the rope, raising their end hand over hand, and beginning Ben's descent. A few seconds later, the pack rat popped out of the suspended ceiling and hung below him, wriggling madly, the gold Super Bowl ring clenched in its jaws.

"Ben Slovak, if you let that poor helpless creature fall, I'll break every bone in your body!" Savannah promised, watching nervously.

Ben was too terrified to reply. If that rope slipped, breaking every bone in his body would happen with or without Savannah.

"Careful, shrimp," Darren brayed. "That's my bank account you're holding."

"In your dreams," seethed Tony.

"The ring goes right back to Dr. Egan," Griffin said emphatically. "It was already stolen by one rat. I'm not giving it to two others."

As he spoke, Griffin lost his grip for a moment, and the rope lurched. Shank hung on, stabilizing Ben's descent. But the pack rat squeaked in fear, and the ring dropped from his mouth.

It fell fifteen feet, hit the floor, and skittered across the cement. It took every ounce of Griffin's willpower not to abandon Ben's rope and lunge for it. Darren, Tony, Savannah, and Melissa scrambled after it. Darren got there first, snatched it up, and headed for the door.

A powerful force grabbed him by the back of the collar and hung on — Shank, with one hand on the rope, and the other on Darren. An instant later, Tony joined the struggle.

"Get *off*!" Still clutching the ring, Darren tore himself loose and barreled for the stairs.

"It belongs to the school!" Griffin cried.

Darren laughed. "Later, losers!"

The words died in his throat. There in the doorway, observing the action, stood Dr. Egan.

29

The Bings' van left a lot of rubber on the road as it screeched into the driveway. Husband and wife hit the walk running and burst in the front door.

"Griffin, get down here this minute!" ordered Mr. Bing.

There was no response. The couple exchanged anguished glances.

Mr. Bing pounded up the stairs, while his wife headed for the basement. She could hear her husband rummaging around the bedrooms. Griffin didn't appear to be there, but he wasn't down here, either.

What had their reckless son gotten himself into this time?

Her eyes fell on the PEMA hub. With a gasp, she

realized that the transmit light was out. That wasn't supposed to happen!

Without thinking, she reached for the reset button.

The principal's red face almost glowed in the subdued light of the furnace room. His emotions seemed so intense Griffin was sure that, when the man exploded, they'd all be showered with acid.

Griffin and Shank lowered Ben back to the floor and watched as Pitch clambered down the boiler to join them so they could face the music as a team. The agitated pack rat shook himself at the end of the fishing line like a dog on a leash.

Still, the principal remained speechless. For some reason, Dr. Evil, who was so quick to jump on his students for the slightest misstep, could not find anything to say about this enormous incident.

At last, Darren broke the silence. "Coach, I got your ring back." He handed it over.

The principal accepted it, but his eyes were on Griffin. "A rat?"

"I can explain. . . ." Griffin managed weakly.

The Man With The Plan was the author of the wildest explanations in history, but as he spoke, he knew that this one was the most outlandish of them all — retainer lost at Savannah's, pack rat finds retainer, pack rat brought to school, pack rat trades retainer for ring. It was the kind of story that your own grandmother wouldn't believe, much less the toughest principal on Long Island.

Dr. Egan remained silent, the muscles in his jaw working furiously as he clenched and unclenched his teeth.

There was the clicking sound of approaching high heels, and Celia White fluttered into the basement. Her hawklike stare raked Griffin and the team. "I knew it! I knew if there was trouble, this bunch would be behind it!" She turned to the principal. "This time they won't be getting off so easily! This time the punishment will fit the crime!"

Dr. Egan wheeled on her suddenly. "If the punishment fit the crime, you'd be thrown off your newspaper, and I'd lose my job. Our crimes are the same. We railroaded Griffin just because of his past." He faced Griffin, his expression open and sincere. "I don't even know what to say to you. I'm *so* sorry. I was stupid and unfair, and I jumped to the wrong conclusion."

Darren was astounded. "You *believed* all that?" he blurted.

"I've been standing here for a few minutes," the principal informed him. "I know exactly who rescued the ring — *and* who tried to steal it." He looked meaningfully at Darren and Tony.

"Well, I don't believe a word of it!" Celia White stormed, her birdlike features glaring and severe. "They're bamboozling you just like they've bamboozled their parents and this whole town. *I'm* the only one who holds them accountable!"

"Innocent people don't have to account for anything," the principal stated firmly. "I'm sure that when I ask Mr. Clancy to look in the ceiling, he'll find a pack rat's nest. At that point, the charges will be dropped. And of course Griffin will come back to school with his friends, where he belongs — *if* he'll have me as his principal."

Griffin nodded ecstatically, too overcome with emotion to speak out loud. Could this be true? Was the nightmare finally over?

The team mobbed him in a frenzied huddle of high fives and bear hugs. Shank awarded him a bone-jarring backslap.

"That's awesome, man," Ben managed, his voice choked up.

"Dodgeball won't be the same without you," added Shank, mussing Griffin's hair.

And there, his face pushed downward by Shank's pistonlike fingers, The Man With The Plan beheld a terrible sight.

The green light on his PEMA anklet was blinking.

30

Griffin watched, horrified, as the warning light turned solid red.

Wild eyed, he checked the modified cell phone on his belt. It was still powered on. "Melissa, what's happening? Why is it doing that?"

Melissa's normally stringy hair stuck out like a static electricity demonstration as she checked the device. "The transmitter is still working," she replied, mystified. "Maybe the hub in your basement rebooted itself somehow."

"My parents!" Griffin exclaimed in true pain. "They must have come home and restarted the hub! Now the cops are on the way to my house — and when they find me gone —"

"But you're off the hook," Ben protested. "Just tell them about the pack rat."

"I'm no lawyer," Shank put in uneasily, "but I don't think you're allowed to break house arrest even if you shouldn't have been on it in the first place."

There was a moment of agonized indecision. Yes, Griffin had been proven innocent. But would Detective Sergeant Vizzini accept that excuse? Had Griffin cleared his name for the Super Bowl ring only to be arrested for a PEMA violation?

The silence was broken by, of all people, Dr. Egan. *"Let's move!"* The principal grabbed Griffin's arm and began to haul him up the basement stairs, running full bore.

Griffin had to scramble to keep pace. "Where are we going?"

"Home!" came the urgent reply. "And fast!"

They hit the main floor just as *Hail Caesar* was letting out. The entire audience, hundreds strong, filled the building.

Dr. Egan did not intend to let the crowd slow his progress. Barking "Excuse us!" and "Coming through!" he dragged Griffin on a full-sprint obstacle course down the hall and out the double doors to the parking lot. He shoved Griffin into the passenger seat of his Hyundai and threw himself behind the wheel.

With the play concluded, there was a long lineup of cars waiting to make the left turn onto Cedar Neck Road. The principal veered away from the jam, jumped the curb, and plowed across the lawn, flattening the school's SAFETY FIRST sign.

"Dr. Egan, what are you doing?"

"I got you into this mess," he replied as the car bumped onto the road, "and I intend to get you out of it. What's your address?"

"Two-thirty-one Poplar. But —"

The principal pressed the pedal to the metal, and they roared down the street at double the posted limit. Griffin gripped the door handle as the Sonata ran a light and screamed across the intersection in a high-speed left turn.

Dr. Egan accelerated, weaving in and out of traffic. Griffin was astounded. He had only seen such aggressive driving in Hollywood car chase scenes. To experience the real thing with stubborn, by-the-book Dr. Evil was simply beyond belief.

"If the police catch us, you'll lose your license for a year!" Griffin protested.

"The only police I'm concerned about," the principal replied with determination, "are the ones on their way to your house — and whether or not we can beat them there."

Sure enough, a siren could be heard not far away. As Dr. Egan blasted through the turn into Griffin's neighborhood, they could make out the reflection of police flashers on the low clouds. It was going to be close.

The Hyundai hurtled onto Poplar Street and fishtailed to a stop in the Bings' driveway. No cops — they'd made it! But as Griffin and his principal exited the Sonata, a squad car wheeled onto the block, lights blazing.

"Quick!" Griffin rasped. "The back way!"

They raced around the side of the house and burst in through the kitchen door.

Mr. and Mrs. Bing were at the counter, pale with worry, cell phones in their hands, awaiting news of their son.

"Griffin, what have you *done*?" his mother moaned.

"I'll explain later!" Dr. Egan puffed. "In a few seconds the police are going to be here, and it's urgent we convince them that Griffin has been home all night!"

And before the Bings could respond to this statement, there was insistent pounding at the front door.

"Police! Open up!" called a familiar voice.

They trooped through the house, and Mr. Bing admitted a very agitated Detective Vizzini.

"I have to tell you folks — I'm blown away. Was I speaking Swahili when I explained how much trouble Griffin would be in if he left the house with that bracelet on? Why is it so hard for you to take me seriously? I'm a sergeant of detectives! With a badge! And a gun . . ."

His voice trailed off as he spied Griffin, comfortably established on the living room couch beside Dr. Egan. His gaze traveled to the PEMA unit on the boy's ankle. The light was solid green.

Vizzini's eyes narrowed. "We received an alarm code from that anklet not five minutes ago. Are you telling me that Griffin has been home the whole time?" He looked from face to silent face.

"Well," Mrs. Bing offered carefully, "I was just in the basement, and I noticed that the transmit light on the hub was out. So I pressed the reset button. Maybe that's what happened." It was the truth — with a few important points left out.

"That makes sense to me," Dr. Egan put in helpfully. "The computers at the school are constantly coughing up strange error messages. Most of the time we just ignore them."

"Maybe," the officer mumbled, unconvinced. "May I ask what you're doing here, sir? Wasn't there a big event at the school tonight?"

The principal nodded. "With all the excitement in the building, we made an amazing discovery." He reached into his pocket and produced Art Blankenship's Super Bowl ring. "It turns out that Griffin didn't take it after all. Believe it or not, a pack rat found Griffin's lost retainer and exchanged it for the ring."

"You can't make this stuff up," added Griffin honestly.

The officer was silent for what seemed like an eternity. Finally, he said, "I guess it's possible it happened that way. But you have to understand that this has gone further than my desk. Griffin's under a judge's order. And it's going to take a judge to lift it."

"That will happen first thing tomorrow," Dr. Egan promised. "You all have my word."

Vizzini turned his attention to Griffin. "In the meantime, the anklet stays on, and you stay put. I'm not even going to ask about that thing on your belt — even though it occurs to me to wonder why a kid who's stuck in the house needs a cell phone." He held up his hand as Griffin opened his mouth to speak. "Uh-uh — not a word. I've got a nose, and it's telling me something smells. But if what the principal says is true, and you're really innocent, I hope you understand that I'm only doing my job."

"I'm the one who has to apologize," Dr. Egan said humbly to Griffin and his parents. "This is entirely my fault. The only thing I offer in my own defense is who could have believed all this was the work of a pack rat? But that's still no excuse for how badly I misjudged you, Griffin."

"Thanks, Dr. Egan." Dr. Evil would never be his favorite person. But Griffin had to give the guy credit for admitting he was wrong.

Later, when Vizzini had gone and Griffin was ushering the principal to the door, Dr. Egan was still contrite. "If there's anything I can do to make this up to you, all you have to do is name it. If it's within my power, I'll make it happen."

Griffin thought it over. "I'm fine with it, Dr. Egan. I just want to get back to my old life. But there's this eighth grader at JFK — Sheldon Brickhaus. You might have noticed him tonight — the big kid with the square head. He's a really good guy, a loyal friend, even though he looks kind of scary. Plus, he's smart — and if he stays at Jail For

Kids, he's never going to make anything out of himself. I'm positive that, if he had a chance to go to our school, he could turn it around."

The principal regarded Griffin with respect, impressed that the boy had asked a favor for a friend, rather than for himself. "I'll see what I can do."

31

The Cedarville Middle School production of *Hail Caesar* received only one review. It was by Celia White in the *Herald*.

She hated it.

According to her, the only saving grace was the performance of the star, Logan Kellerman, who showed "poise and professionalism under the worst circumstances any actor could ever possibly face."

She also mentioned that this would be her final column for the *Herald*. After thirty years, she was quitting to write a book. It was to be a work of nonfiction, chronicling the legal battle of the Bartholomew family suing the Cedarville School District over the ownership of Art Blankenship's Super Bowl ring.

Dr. Egan vowed to fight the lawsuit all the way to the Supreme Court. In his opinion, too many people had suffered over that ring for the school to give it up.

"I appreciate your coming with me, Griffin," said Mr. Bing, pulling the van to a stop in the dirt parking lot of the orchard. "I'm going to need all the moral support I can get today."

"I'm glad it worked out, Dad." Griffin hitched up his pant leg and examined the pink skin above his ankle where the PEMA bracelet had once been.

This trip — to accompany his father on the field test of the Vole-B-Gone — was his first outing after the official lifting of his house arrest. Even with Dr. Egan pleading his case, it hadn't been easy to convince Judge Koretsky that the entire Super Bowl ring incident had been a misunderstanding. She had even demanded to see the pack rat in question. Luckily, the light-fingered rodent had not been difficult to find. The Drysdales had adopted him. He was the current pride of Savannah's menagerie, with his own cage and a new name: Arthur — after Art Blankenship, assistant linebacker coach of the New York Jets team that won it all so many years ago. Resplendent in his rodent harness, Arthur went on long walks with Savannah and Luthor, whose confinement had been lifted by animal control — so long as he was kept at least five hundred feet away from football fields.

Mr. Bing's face was careworn as he popped the hatch and removed the Vole-B-Gone prototype. "Who am I kidding? I can't make this thing work."

"It works great, Dad," Griffin amended. "It isn't your fault the voles stay away."

"Then it might as well not work at all," his father said, totally discouraged.

Griffin surveyed the vast property, thousands of fruit trees planted in tight rows along rolling hills that stretched as far as the eye could see. Man, it was nice to be out in the open! He hadn't realized how cooped up he'd felt under house arrest.

"How do we know this orchard even has voles?" he asked. "We can't very well catch them if they aren't here."

His father shook his head sadly. "This place has suffered vole damage for decades. There are voles, all right. The problem is my prototype. It was a mistake from the start. And after the test, my investors are going to know it."

Griffin flashed him an encouraging smile. "Think positive, Dad. I have a gut feeling about today."

A gleaming black SUV roared into the parking lot. Mr. Bing let out a nervous breath. "Let me greet my investors." He handed the Vole-B-Gone to Griffin. "Wish me luck!"

"Luck's got nothing to do with it," Griffin said confidently.

As soon as his father's back was turned, he pulled Shank's bottle of Rendezvous in Paris out of his pocket. Hefting the prototype, he sprayed generous shots of the sickening-sweet perfume on the bait station, the floor of the trap, and, for good measure, the bars of the cage.

Wrinkling his nose from the powerful stink, Griffin looked around. A pair of beady black eyes had already appeared in the dry brush that ringed the parking lot, gazing hungrily up at the Vole-B-Gone. Moments later, a second vole poked out of the grass, followed by a third. Tiny pink noses sniffed excitedly at the bewitching aroma of Rendezvous in Paris.

Perfect. Three voles, and the trap hadn't even been set yet. By the time this demonstration was over, they were going to be lined up to get in.

There were advantages to being friends with the son of a nuisance wildlife removal expert.

Poor Mom and Dad had suffered mightily being the parents of The Man With The Plan. Griffin wanted to do everything he could to make it up to them.

Sheldon Brickhaus did not squander his opportunity to get out of Jail For Kids and enroll at Cedarville Middle School. He was not a straight-A student, but he kept his grades up and his nose clean. With encouragement from Dr. Egan, he even joined the football team.

Shank had never played football before, so his skills were mediocre in every area but one. His talent for bone-jarring tackles turned out to be as impressive as his talent for dodgeball. Suddenly, the Cedarville Seahawks had the most feared linebacker in the county.

The score was tied 7–7 in a misty, muddy home game when Shank forced a fumble and brought the Seahawks offense back onto the field.

Coach Egan tapped Darren Vader on the helmet. Darren jumped up eagerly. He had been riding the bench a lot since his attempt to make off with the Super Bowl ring on the night of *Hail Caesar.*

Amid the wind, rain, and crowd noise, no one noticed that, when Darren tried to take the field, Shank wrapped him up with powerful arms and drove him backward into a stand of bushes. Nor did anyone detect that the Seahawk who took Darren's place in the lineup was a lot shorter and smaller than the player who normally wore number 23.

The ball was snapped and handed off to the newcomer. Number 23 blasted through the phalanx of defenders, sidestepping tacklers and leaping athletically over blockers. By the time the runner reached daylight, a burst of blazing speed left every other player on both teams standing still in the mud.

"Wow!" Coach Egan exclaimed in amazement. "When did Vader get so fast?"

Number 23 streaked the length of the field and crossed the goal line with an acrobatic front flip, spiking the ball with a mighty splash. The home crowd roared its approval.

Basking in triumph, the ball carrier ripped off the Seahawks helmet and threw it high in the air.

Down cascaded long honey blond hair. It was Pitch Benson, at last living the football glory that had been kept from her.

All at once, the thunderous crowd noise was replaced by shocked silence. The only cheering now was coming from the thicket, where Griffin, Ben, Shank, Savannah, Logan, and Melissa held the real Darren — minus his jersey — captive.

"I got mugged!" Darren wailed.

The referee blew his whistle, disallowing the touchdown, and the scoreboard operator scrambled to take the six points away from the Seahawks. Pitch ran off the field before she could be thrown off, joining the celebration in the thicket.

Dr. Egan shot a furious look in their direction, but the blizzard of high fives continued.

Sure, Griffin thought, it was probably stupid to risk trouble so soon after the last time. But it served Darren right. And who was entitled to this moment more than Pitch, after being shut out of the team?

If there was one lesson being framed had taught Griffin, it was that he was surrounded by the greatest people on the face of the earth. Back when all the evidence had been against him, Ben, Pitch, Savannah, Melissa, Logan, and, in the end, Shank had never given up on him. Not even when he'd given up on himself.

Griffin Bing believed in planning 100 percent. But there was something more important than having the right plan.

It was having the right friends.